"What have we done, Nate?"

Hallie pushed herself up on her elbow to look at him.

"What we should have done a long time ago."

"To get each other out of our systems, you mean?"

He kept his eyes closed when he said, "I'll never get you out of my system, Hallie."

"Nor you, mine, Nate. But that really doesn't change the situation, does it?"

He opened his eyes and sat up, resting his back against the headboard. "No. It doesn't."

Hallie sat up, too, bringing her knees to her chest as she pulled the sheet up around her. "Do you really think that I haven't thought about what it would be like if we kept Ahn?"

Dear Reader,

As a parent and a grandparent, the parenting role is naturally near and dear to my heart. *A Ranch Called Home* was my tribute to the single mom. And in *Dad's E-mail Order Bride* I paid homage to the single dad.

In my third Harlequin Superromance, however, I wanted to explore a different side of parenting. I've always had the utmost admiration for people who open their hearts and adopt a child. But it wasn't until I began thinking about writing an adoption story that I realized I'd never given much thought to the other side of the adoption coin— the unselfishness involved in putting a child's best interest first.

Adopted Parents addresses that issue. And as I began writing the story from the aunt and uncle's point of view, I began to understand that loving a child enough to do the right thing is just as important as loving a child enough to become a parent.

I hope you enjoy reading Hallie and Nate's story as they struggle through a tragedy to find true love. I love to hear from readers, so please visit my Web site at www.CandyHalliday.com.

Best always,

Candy Halliday

Adopted Parents
Candy Halliday

HARLEQUIN®

TORONTO • NEW YORK • LONDON
AMSTERDAM • PARIS • SYDNEY • HAMBURG
STOCKHOLM • ATHENS • TOKYO • MILAN • MADRID
PRAGUE • WARSAW • BUDAPEST • AUCKLAND

Recycling programs
for this product may
not exist in your area.

ISBN-13: 978-0-373-71664-7

ADOPTED PARENTS

Printed in U.S.A.

ABOUT THE AUTHOR

Romance author Candy Halliday lives in the Piedmont of North Carolina with her husband, a spastic schnauzer named Millie and an impossible attack cat named Flash. Candy's daughter and son-in-law and her two teenage grandchildren live nearby. Candy loves to hear from readers. Visit her on the Web at www.candyhalliday.com.

Don't miss any of our special offers. Write to us at the following address for information on our newest releases.

Harlequin Reader Service
U.S.: 3010 Walden Ave., P.O. Box 1325, Buffalo, NY 14269
Canadian: P.O. Box 609, Fort Erie, Ont. L2A 5X3

This book is dedicated to the loving parents
who give adopted children a second chance—
and to those who step aside to make it possible.

ACKNOWLEDGMENTS

Special thanks to my super agent, Jenny Bent.

Extreme thanks to my amazing editor,
Wanda Ottewell.

Love and thanks always to my incredible family:
Blue, Shelli, Tracy, Quint and Caroline.

CHAPTER ONE

IN A PERFECT WORLD there would be no tragic news that your sister and brother-in-law had been in a fatal car accident. No baby left behind. No difficult decisions to be made about the child's future.

But the world wasn't perfect.

No one knew that better than Hallie Weston.

The past three weeks had been a nightmare, her emotions spinning so fast Hallie felt trapped inside a revolving door. Disbelief. Inconsolable grief. Blind anger at the drunk driver who had taken Janet and David from her. Back to disbelief again.

At the moment, all Hallie felt was numb.

She was sitting in the boardroom of her dead brother-in-law's law practice, waiting for a Monday morning meeting with David's partner, Greg Holder, and all Hallie kept thinking was how adamant David had been six months ago about tying up loose ends after he and Janet adopted their daughter, Ahn. Hallie had believed then that David was simply in his usual attorney mode, dotting his *i*'s and crossing his *t*'s when he'd produced the joint guardianship document for her and his brother Nate to sign at the baby's christening.

Now Hallie had to wonder.

Had David somehow sensed that he and Janet wouldn't live to finish the journey they started with the precious baby girl they'd brought back from Vietnam? Had Nate wondered the same thing?

And even though Nate sat right beside her it wasn't a question Hallie would ask.

Because every woman had a guy from her past whom she'd made a complete fool of herself over. Nathan Brock happened to be that guy for Hallie.

Ten years later, she still hadn't forgiven him.

She'd been only twenty-one then, fresh out of college, and willing to take a peon's job in order to get her foot in the door at Boston's top television station. Nate had been thirty—a gorgeous, confident older guy Hallie couldn't resist. He'd also been her boss, the TV station's shining star, and already on his way to becoming the award-winning photojournalist he was today.

She'd fallen for Nate hard and fast.

The admiration had *not* been mutual.

After only one week of working as Nate's gofer, he'd transferred her to the production department. And he'd told Hallie if she really intended to make it in television she needed to focus on her career and drop the silly schoolgirl crushes.

His smack-down had been cold and swift.

The humiliation had crushed her young ego.

Had Hallie not dragged Janet to Nate's going-away party for moral support when he got his first big break with CNN, they wouldn't be together in this boardroom now. Nate's brother David had also been at the party and their siblings had the instant sparks that Nate and Hallie never had. After Hallie's big sister married Nate's little brother, they settled into a polite disregard for each other.

Just as they were doing now.

Sitting in silence, carefully not engaging.

From the corner of her eye Hallie saw Nate's arm come up to check his watch again. It didn't surprise her when he rose and walked to the other side of the boardroom.

Nate had always been a restless spirit. He'd never been tied down to any one person or any one place, and Hallie doubted he ever would be. She studied him as he stood at the window staring out at downtown Boston from their tenth-floor advantage.

Damn him.

He was still the sexiest man Hallie had ever seen.

Everything about him said one hundred percent male. Tall. Broad shoulders. Sun-streaked hair that curled just above his collar. Even the way he was standing oozed masculinity—hands at the waist of his khaki pants, his blue dress shirtsleeves rolled up, exposing strong arms Hallie had once dreamed of having around her.

She sighed and looked away.

The reflection in the glass walls of the boardroom made Hallie gasp. The woman staring back at her looked horrible. There were ugly dark circles under her eyes. Her short black hair looked lifeless. And the tailored dress that had once fit now hung on her like a sack.

Hallie reached up and pinched her cheeks, trying to bring a little color back into her face. It didn't help. Running her fingers through her hair didn't improve her looks, either. The spiked effect only made her look even more like some homeless stray who had wandered in off the streets wearing someone else's clothes.

Even sadder, that was how Hallie felt.

Janet and David's home had been her go-to place, where she'd always celebrated her birthday, and the holidays, or any other special occasion. There she'd gone if she needed comfort, or advice, or just to unwind and get out of Boston for the weekend. Where she'd never needed an invitation and where she'd always felt welcome. And now what had made that house her soft place to land was gone.

So of course she felt homeless. Her life would never be the same again.

She glanced at Nate, still standing at the window with the same fatigued look on his face that Hallie had seen on hers only a few seconds ago. *How tragic,* she thought, *the games people play.*

They were both devastated, both hurting, yet they couldn't even comfort each other thanks to something stupid that had happened ten years ago. Hallie was tempted to get up, walk over to Nate, and tell him he could cry on her shoulder the way she so desperately needed to cry on his.

Maybe then the screaming in her head would stop.

She wouldn't, of course, walk over and tell Nate anything. Hallie hadn't even thanked him yet for taking charge once he'd arrived home from his current assignment in Afghanistan.

Nate had taken care of everything she couldn't.

He'd made funeral arrangements she was in no shape to make. He'd handled the endless details the crisis had created. He'd spoken with well-wishing family members and friends Hallie couldn't bring herself to face.

Nate had given her time to pull herself together—something she was pretty sure she hadn't yet accomplished.

And the hardest part was knowing she'd survive.

Somehow, she'd have to learn to live with the loss. Someway, she'd have to find the strength to move on. And someday, maybe the pain inside her chest wouldn't hurt so much it took her breath away.

"Sorry I've kept you waiting," Greg Holder said as he hurried into the boardroom.

He paused by Hallie's chair long enough to give her shoulder a supportive squeeze. Next, he shook hands with Nate, who had approached the table when Greg entered.

Greg was a handsome guy, in his late thirties and blond. He was dressed the way a successful attorney should dress: designer suit, tasteful tie, expensive loafers. He'd been David's college roommate and best friend. He was also the executor of David's and Janet's wills.

Knowing Greg personally was a comfort to Hallie. It took some of the sting out of the unpleasantness that had brought them here this morning.

"I know this is hard for both of you," Greg said as he took a seat across the table from them and placed a large folder in front of him. "And the last thing I ever wanted to do was act as executor of my best friend's will. But the sooner we settle David and Janet's affairs and set the wheels in motion to find new parents for Ahn, the better it will be for everyone."

Hallie gave Greg a brave nod.

Nate said, "I agree."

Greg opened the folder, then looked at both of them. "The wills are identical, as is the case with most husbands and wives. And I want to go over the will provisions first because this is always the hardest part for the family."

He paused, sympathy for both of them evident on his face. "No one ever wants to benefit financially from a loved one's death. But I hope you will accept David's and Janet's final wishes in the spirit in which they were given. Out of their love and their concern for your well-being and your future."

Hallie swallowed past the lump in her throat.

But she didn't cry.

She didn't have any tears left.

"You are the two main beneficiaries, and everything is to be divided equally between the two of you," Greg said. "There are three exceptions. A trust fund for Ahn's college education that the firm will manage until Ahn reaches legal age. A trust fund the firm will also manage to pay for your mother's care at the nursing facility, Nate. And a monetary gift to Hallie and

Janet's stepmother. I'll discuss the details with Roberta later."

Roberta was taking care of Ahn this morning so Nate and Hallie could have this meeting.

Greg pushed a sheet of paper across the table.

"This is an itemized list of the assets."

Hallie only half listened as Greg rambled on about Janet and David's house in Winchester on Wedge Pond. About their personal property. About their investment and retirement accounts and their life insurance. About the proceeds Janet had received when she'd sold her accounting firm so she could be a stay-at-home mom. About David's equity in the law practice.

She looked at the paper when Greg's finger finally reached the bottom of the sheet. "This is the total amount of all assets," he said, "with the exception of the insurance settlement from the accident. Beside your name is the amount that represents your half of the inheritance after necessary taxes."

Hallie stared at the figure beside her name. The 2.5-million-dollar amount was staggering.

She'd never given a thought to Janet and David's net worth before. She'd known they were successful. But their finances hadn't been any of her business.

"It's in your best interest if we don't settle with the other driver's insurance company until after the readoption," Greg said. "If we can't find adoptive parents and one of you ends up raising Ahn, the settlement needs to reflect the expenses you'll incur in taking care of her until she's out of college and on her own."

Hallie panicked. She couldn't even consider the idea of raising Ahn. "But readoption is what Janet and David wanted. They were adamant about that. They wanted Ahn raised by *two* parents who could give her the same stability they were giving her. It states that plainly in the guardianship agreement."

"And I'll do everything possible to make the readoption happen," Greg said. "But Ahn's age and her delayed speech and physical development could be an issue. Most couples want an infant instead of a toddler. And frankly, any type of disability makes a child less adoptable."

Hallie was reeling over this reality. She and Nate weren't parent material and Janet and David had known that. In fact, she and Nate were as far from parent material as any two people could be.

Nate's life was devoted to the dangerous assignments he accepted wherever trouble was brewing in the world. And she *had* focused on her career. Her position as an executive television producer required one hundred percent of her time.

If either of them had a spouse, Janet and David might have felt differently about their prospects for raising Ahn. But Hallie couldn't even boast a significant other at the moment. And unless Nate had someone hidden in the background, he had no one special in his life, either.

They were both married to their careers.

Definitely *not* parent material.

But Hallie had been sister material. And she was aunt

material. And since they were now talking about the readoption, Hallie decided to bring up something that had been bothering her. "What if I want to maintain contact with Ahn? Is that even a possibility?"

Nate looked at her, his gray eyes zooming in on Hallie like the lens of one of his fancy cameras. "And why would you want to do that?"

Hallie wasn't surprised he would disagree. She and Nate never agreed on anything. "Because she's my niece," Hallie said simply. "And *yours*," she added for spite.

"And if she were older," Nate said, "I would agree with you. But Ahn's only two, and David and Janet were her parents for six short months. She isn't going to remember them, much less you or me. She needs to bond with her new parents. She doesn't need any interference from us."

His reference to Ahn's age hit home.

Hallie had been two years older than Ahn when her mother died of breast cancer, yet any personal memories of her mother were vague at best. But what she did have were the memories Janet had shared with her.

Janet, who had been eight when their mother died, had been her memory keeper.

And though Janet never intended for Hallie to raise Ahn, it only seemed right that Ahn should have a memory keeper, too. Hallie was determined to remain Ahn's aunt so Ahn would never doubt how much Janet loved her.

"If you can pretend Ahn never existed after the

readoption, good for you," Hallie told Nate. "But I can't. I don't intend to interfere in her life, but I don't like the idea of handing her over to strangers without keeping tabs on her. I owe Janet that much."

"That's guilt talking over reason, Hallie," Nate said.

"Maybe," Hallie admitted. "But now that Greg told us about Ahn's trust fund I feel even more strongly about staying in touch with her. Someone has to look out for her interests."

Greg cleared his throat. "I should have made myself clear about the trust fund. The adoptive parents won't have access to that money. Only Ahn can access it when she reaches legal age."

"I'm not worried about the money, Greg," Hallie said. "I'm trying to point out that eventually Ahn *will* know that Janet and David were her first adoptive parents. Don't you think she'll wonder why Janet and David's family didn't care enough about her to stay in touch?"

"Again," Nate said, "you're letting your heart over-rule your head. David and Janet knew all you and I had to offer this child was choosing the best possible parents to raise her. Don't intrude on Ahn's life to ease your conscience. An occasional call or a card now and then, and birthday and Christmas presents aren't worth it."

Hallie felt like slapping him.

He'd lectured her once, but those days were over. What she did was none of Nate's damn business!

Hallie turned to Greg. "If Nate doesn't want to

maintain contact with Ahn after the readoption, that's his prerogative. But I intend to remain a part of Ahn's life, regardless of how small that part is."

"Then you need to be prepared that finding parents who agree to that condition might add another stumbling block to the process," Greg said. "Most adoptive parents prefer no major ties with the child's past."

"I'm prepared to take that chance."

"How much of a stumbling block?" Nate asked.

Greg shrugged. "There's no way of knowing until we start interviewing parents and see if Hallie maintaining contact is a deal breaker."

"And if it's a deal breaker," Hallie said with confidence, "that's my proof they aren't the right parents."

She looked back at Nate for his comeback.

A muscle in his jaw twitched, but Nate dropped the subject.

Greg pushed another document toward them. "This is a form from the private adoption agency we'll be working with that specifies the requirements a couple must meet before you'll consider them as parents. That's why I asked you to meet with Deb Langston this morning. She'll help you fill out the questionnaire and you can drop it off with my assistant after your appointment. The agency can't begin screening parents until they have the information."

Hallie reached out, picked up the questionnaire and placed it in her purse. But she was dreading their next appointment even more than she'd dreaded this one.

Dr. Deborah Langston was the child psychologist

Janet and David had been working with since the adoption to help Ahn acclimate to her new surroundings. What worried Hallie was Dr. Langston picking up on the underlying tension between her and Nate.

Hallie was in no mood to do any explaining. And she knew that went double for Nate.

Nate wasn't the talk-it-all-out type. His guard was always up like some badge of honor—never letting anyone too close, hanging back and keeping his distance. He'd even been that way with David to a certain extent, although David had never let Nate get away with it.

Hallie couldn't count the number of times she'd seen David grab Nate in a bear hug and tell his brother he loved him. Nate had always grimaced and never hugged back. But Hallie knew Nate loved his brother.

He obviously had issues but they were his.

Hallie had her own emotional issues to worry about. The next few months were going to be horrific, and the last thing Hallie needed was some psychologist probing into the complex nature of their relationship. She was one second away from asking Greg if he could have the psychologist fill out the questionnaire without a meeting being necessary when Greg glanced at his watch.

"It's only nine-thirty," he said. "You'll have a few minutes to grab a cup of coffee in the lobby if you want." He pushed a business card forward. "I made your appointment for ten o'clock. Dr. Langston's office is on the sixth floor. That's her suite number."

Greg stood, picked up his folder and circled the table.

He shook hands with Nate who stood as well. "Just remember," he said, "Ahn is the real victim here. Her best interest has to come first."

Those words made Hallie wince.

What a selfish, hypocritical bitch she was. She'd just debated with Nate, spouting her concern for Ahn, when she hadn't been thinking about Ahn at all. She'd only been thinking about herself. And yes, as Nate accused, trying to soothe her guilty conscience.

It killed Hallie knowing she hadn't spent more time with Janet and Ahn while Janet was alive. She'd been too busy. Too busy to spend time with the sister she loved and the niece she didn't even know. If only she could turn back the clock.

If only.

Greg's hand rested on Hallie's shoulder again. "Don't worry, we'll find the right parents. Call me if you need anything. Otherwise, I'll be in touch when I have potential couples for you to interview."

We'll find the right parents.

How Hallie prayed that was true.

She was Ahn's aunt. She was never meant to be her mother. But she'd be a better aunt than mere calls and cards and presents as Nate accused. She'd be there for Ahn, just as Janet had always been there for Hallie. And her heart overruling her head had nothing to do with it.

It was the right thing to do.

CHAPTER TWO

WHEN THEY WALKED into the elevator and Hallie pushed the button for the sixth floor, Nate knew they would *not* be going down to the lobby for coffee before their meeting as Greg suggested. But that was okay.

Flying under the radar was Nate's main goal.

He'd been trying to keep the peace. And he'd been trying to avoid as much confrontation with Hallie as possible from the moment he'd arrived in Boston.

It hadn't been easy.

One minute Nate was amazed at Hallie's resolve, the next minute he wanted to shake her. She'd blindsided him when she'd told Greg she wanted to stay in touch with Ahn.

That was the first he'd heard of it.

And she'd certainly had plenty of time to tell him.

Hallie had been in his face for the past week trying to dictate what they were going to do about Ahn until they could find new parents. As far as Nate was concerned, that issue was still unresolved. He wasn't sure what part of *joint* guardian Hallie didn't understand, but he was real close to patiently explaining it to her.

Still, Nate feared he was going to lose the battle.

For years Hallie had pretended to tolerate him for David and Janet's sake. He knew it. She knew it. But there was no reason to tolerate him now. And Hallie had made it exceedingly clear all she wanted from him was him to be *gone*.

She'd told him flat out to go back to Afghanistan.

There was no reason for him to stay, she'd said. *She* would hire a full-time nanny for Ahn, and *she* would stay at David and Janet's until they could find new parents. And since both of them had to agree, when she did find a couple she liked, *then* he could fly home, interview them and see if they met his approval.

There was only one problem with Hallie's plan.

Nate wasn't going back to Afghanistan.

Had Hallie given him the chance—instead of barking out orders at him—he would have told her that he'd arranged for his replacement even before he left for the States. But then, Nate had run out of chances with Hallie a long time ago.

He glanced over his shoulder at her standing behind him in the elevator. Her arms were folded, her head resting back against the elevator wall, her eyes closed.

She was tired, just as he was. Tired of the mind-numbing pain. Tired of the difficult task before them. Tired of knowing their lives had changed forever.

She'd always been on the thin side, but since the funeral Hallie seemed to be melting away before Nate's eyes. If she weighed much more than one hundred pounds, Nate would be shocked.

He was worried about her.

Nate knew how grief had the power to ravish the human soul. He'd seen it happen to his mother after his father was killed rescuing a fellow firefighter. Nate couldn't remember a time growing up when his mother hadn't been depressed. She was in a nursing home now way before her time, her chronic depression finally leading to Alzheimer's disease, which had put her there.

At least she'd been spared David's death because now his mother didn't remember her sons at all.

It worried Nate that he could see the same thing happening to Hallie—letting her grief consume her, falling into a deep depression. And it didn't matter that she had a satisfying career or that she enjoyed her life as a single woman. All that faded with these horrific circumstances they faced.

Nate knew Janet had been Hallie's touchstone—the glue that held Hallie's life together. Hallie had said those exact words five years ago. Not to him, of course. She'd been talking to David while the three of them sat in the hospital waiting room after Janet had been rushed into emergency surgery for the ectopic pregnancy that sadly ended her ability to have children.

Nate had never forgotten the lost look on Hallie's face as she sat there for hours worrying about her sister. And how could he? He'd been seeing that same lost look on Hallie's face from the moment he got home.

That was why he was positive no good could come from Hallie living in Wedge Pond where she was constantly reminded that the one person she'd always depended on was gone. *He* should be the one to stay at

David and Janet's and hire a full-time nanny to take
care of Ahn. Hallie needed to come back to her apartment here in Boston and go back to work as soon as
possible.

She needed to be in her own element. Keeping busy.
Being productive. Handling her daily executive producer
problems that were constantly coming at her from all
directions.

Busy was good.

Busy helped keep the pain at bay.

Besides, did it really matter who stayed to supervise
the nanny? The nanny would be taking care of Ahn,
just as Roberta had been caring for the child since the
accident. In fact, Nate couldn't think of one time Hallie
had even held Ahn over the past few weeks, much less
taken any responsibility for her care. But he wasn't
being fair—he'd made no attempt to interact with Ahn,
either.

Since the accident, it had taken everything he and
Hallie had to put one foot in front of the other and make
it through another day. Allowing Roberta to ease the
burden by caring for the baby had been what anyone
would have done under the circumstances.

Thinking about Hallie's stepmother, however, sent
Nate's thoughts in a different direction. As soon as he
had an opportunity to talk to her alone, he needed to
win Roberta over to his way of thinking.

Roberta had a lot of influence over Hallie even if
they did butt heads on a regular basis. If Roberta sided
with him, eventually maybe Hallie would, too.

The bell dinged and the elevator doors opened.

Nate stepped aside and politely motioned for Hallie to go ahead of him. She stared at him for a second before she shifted her purse strap to her shoulder and stepped forward. Nate was *not* prepared when Hallie suddenly grabbed his arm and marched him into the hallway.

"We need to talk before this meeting."

She pointed to the unisex restroom directly across from the elevator. The next thing Nate knew, they were in the tiny bathroom together with the door locked. Hallie had her back against the door as if to prevent his escape.

So much for flying under the radar.

There was no getting along with this woman.

"Talk about what?" Nate demanded.

"You know exactly about what," she said. "What we should have talked about ten years ago. We should have had it out back then and gotten it over with."

Nate frowned. "And that's what you want to do now? Stand here in a public bathroom and finally have it out?" He hoped she would see how ridiculous that sounded.

The determined look on her face said she didn't.

"That's exactly what I want to do," she said. "We're minutes away from meeting with a psychologist. If we don't put our differences to rest before this meeting, we're both going to end up in therapy."

"Fine," Nate said, throwing his hands up in the air. "You want to have it out, Hallie? Go for it. Blast away."

She crossed her arms. "That Friday night after my

first week at the station when we all went out for drinks after work at the club. Tell me the truth. If you weren't interested in me, Nate, why did you insist on taking me home?"

Nate's laugh was cynical. "You mean *after* you took your blouse off on the dance floor?"

Her chin came up. "I was hot and I had a camisole on *underneath* my blouse and you know it. In fact, even without it, I was wearing more than most women in that club."

"Then maybe it was the way you twirled your blouse around over your head like a stripper before you threw it into the crowd. Yeah. I'm pretty sure that's when I realized you'd had a little too much to drink and it might be wise if I made sure you got home safe."

"Safe?" She snorted. "I sure wouldn't call what we were doing in the back of that taxi any kind of *safe*. If I remember right, we were all over each other."

"I'd had my share of alcohol that night, too," Nate said in his own defense.

One eyebrow came up when she said, "But you were sober on Saturday when you went to see the station manager to have me transferred, Nate. And that's what I've never understood. Why didn't you just call me and tell me you weren't interested in me? Why did you let me walk into the station on Monday morning when everyone knew we'd left the bar together Friday night and embarrass me like that?"

Nate let out a long sigh and ran a hand through his hair as he tried to sort out what he wanted to say. And yes, he was stalling. And who wouldn't? He was trapped in a bathroom with a woman who had been seething for ten long years over what he'd done to her.

Nate could tell the truth.

Or he could lie about it.

Either way, he doubted Hallie would ever be satisfied.

Nate opted for the truth. "You were a kid, Hallie. You were too young for me. But I knew if we continued working together, we would end up in bed. That left me with two choices, and both of them sucked. I could be a jerk and sleep with you. Or I could be a jerk and have you transferred. I did what I thought was best for you under the circumstances. And that's the honest truth."

IT WAS THE LAST THING Hallie had expected Nate to say.

And the worst thing Nate could have admitted.

She couldn't even take any satisfaction in his admission that he *had* been attracted to her—which came as a shock to Hallie. Maybe that satisfaction would come later. But at the moment, Hallie was pissed.

"And you couldn't have told me I was too young for you? To back off? That it wasn't going to happen between us?" Hallie demanded. "You really thought destroying my self-esteem and humiliating me in front of everyone at the station was the best thing you could do for me? Under the circumstances?"

"I guess this is the wrong time to point out that

transferring you to the production department actually worked out pretty well for you."

Hallie's eyes narrowed. "Don't you dare make light of what you did to me, Nate. I won't stand for it. Everyone thought we slept together, even though we didn't. And that left me looking like the stupid bimbo you tossed aside after you got what you wanted."

His expression softened. "You're right," he said. "I shouldn't have embarrassed you like that. And I should have apologized to you a long time ago."

"Then why didn't you?"

Nate kept staring at her.

Hallie stared back. In fact, it felt good staring openly at Nate like this, instead of one of them doing what they usually did and looking away if their eyes happened to meet.

Maybe too good.

"Let me ask you this," Nate said. "What if I had apologized to you after I had you transferred? And what if I'd told you the truth that I thought you were too young for me? Would you have backed off and accepted the fact that it wasn't going to happen between us?"

He caught Hallie off guard with those questions.

She thought of all the times she'd brought a date to Thanksgiving dinner, or to Christmas, or to any other function at Janet and David's when she knew Nate was going to be there. It had been her way of thumbing her nose at Nate's rejection, her proof that other men desired her whether Nate did or not.

Over the years, she'd dated more men, she'd broken

up with more men and she'd turned down more men than she cared to remember. And the sad truth was, not one of them measured up to this man.

But did she have the guts to 'fess up and tell him the truth?

"Yes, I would have accepted your apology," Hallie finally said. "But no, I wouldn't have backed off. I was crazy about you. I would have pursued you to the depths of hell and back trying to prove you wrong."

"And that's why I had you transferred," Nate said. "I knew I couldn't survive another taxi ride."

Hallie sighed and shook her head. "And all these years I thought the very sight of me disgusted you. That you were an insufferable egotistical bastard who didn't think I was worthy of your time."

"The very sight of me *did* disgust you," he mentioned.

Hallie grimaced at the thought of how rude she'd been to Nate so many times. "I'm so sorry, Nate."

"So am I," he said. "For *everything*."

It was his inflection on *everything* that got her.

The *everything* currently eating them both up inside.

Hallie stepped forward, and slid her arms around Nate's waist, letting her head rest on his shoulder. She felt him stiffen for a second, but he put his arms around her, too.

There was nothing sexual about their embrace. Nothing sexual implied. Nothing sexual intended. Nothing sexual period. Their embrace was completely innocent, but it was long overdue.

They simply held each other.

No words were necessary.

No words were adequate for the loss they'd suffered.

But having Nate's arms around her was the comfort Hallie had been waiting for since the two policemen arrived at her office to tell her about the accident. Comfort from the one person who loved Janet and David every bit as much as she did.

CHAPTER THREE

BY THE TIME she and Nate made it to Dr. Deborah Langston's office, Hallie had stopped worrying about the psychologist picking up on any underlying tension between them. The heart-to-heart in the bathroom had altered the dynamics of their strained relationship.

But the emotional upheaval had been exhausting.

All Hallie wanted was to go back to Wedge Pond so she could retreat and not have to talk to anyone else for the remainder of the day. Then she'd have time to take stock. Ahn, Nate, and Roberta were the only family she had left. But there were no blood ties to keep them together. Janet and David had been their bond. Without that center pulling them all in, would they keep in touch? Given how Hallie had never really gotten along with Roberta, it was doubtful. And she'd truly be alone.

So if she didn't want that, it was up to her to strengthen those relationships. How the hell she'd accomplish that baffled her at the moment. And the mere thought of no family to catch her when she fell nearly brought her to her knees.

Hallie took a deep breath when Nate opened the

office door. First things first. Get through this interview, then she could figure out how to hold three fiercely independent souls together.

"I hope this won't take long." She looked around thinking the reception room was exactly what she expected—a kid-friendly section in one corner, reception-style chairs lining the walls. The pleasant surprise, however, was that no one else was waiting. That gave Hallie hope there would be no delays seeing Dr. Langston.

Nate followed as she walked toward the closed glass window where an older woman with frosted hair and dark-rimmed glasses was sitting talking on the phone. The woman ignored them completely until she finally ended the call. She slid the glass window open without saying a word, the bored expression on her face broadcasting how much she hated her job.

"Hallie Weston and Nate Brock to see Dr. Langston," Hallie told her. "We have a ten-o'clock appointment."

She picked up a clipboard and shoved it through the window at Hallie. "Take a seat and fill this out."

Hallie refused to take it. "We're only here to talk to Dr. Langston about one of her patients."

"I still need your insurance information to bill for the consult fee."

"I don't intend to file the consult on my insurance," Hallie told her. "I'll pay cash for the consult fee."

She gave Hallie a condescending look. "I *still* need your information in order to give you a receipt. Take a seat and fill out the form."

Nate finally reached out and took the clipboard.

The woman slammed the window with a bang.

"I wasn't trying to be difficult," Hallie whispered as Nate led her to a group of chairs as far from the window as possible. "But there was no excuse for her being so rude."

"Don't worry about it," he said as they both sat. "I can fill out the information."

Hallie was too tired to argue with him.

She watched as Nate opened the clip to remove the pen and began filling out the form. She really didn't know why she'd been so confrontational a few minutes ago, other than the woman's outright rudeness.

Maybe it was being out in the public for the first time in weeks. Having to actually deal with people when all she wanted to do was climb into bed, pull the covers over her head and shut the world out completely.

Or maybe she was losing it.

She sure felt as though she could snap at any minute. And if something as simple as filling out a form took her to the edge, what little thing would actually push her over?

Hallie's grim thoughts were interrupted by a drop-dead gorgeous blonde calling out their names. Nate was on his feet so fast he almost dropped the clipboard.

Not that Hallie could blame him.

The blonde's hair fell soft around her shoulders, and her clothes certainly weren't hanging off her—glued to her was more like it. Her short white skirt hit her well above the knee, and her low-cut turquoise blouse showed off a healthy cleavage.

Dr. Langston obviously needed a few tips on hiring a professional staff. She had a witch for a receptionist and a call girl look-alike for an assistant.

"This way, please." The blonde flashed Nate a bleached-white smile when he handed over the clipboard and then sashayed down the hallway ahead of them. For Nate's benefit, of course. A woman didn't walk that way unless she knew a man was watching.

And Hallie should know. She'd done it too many times to count.

"Here we are." The blonde motioned them inside an open office door to the two chairs facing a desk with Dr. Langston's nameplate. Hallie was about to ask how long they'd have to wait for the doctor when the blonde sat across the desk.

Hallie amended her earlier assessment of the business lessons Dr. Langston needed. Someone should instruct her on appropriate attire and remind her that her clients were not a dating pool she could dip into whenever she wanted. Hallie caught another blinding smile the doctor sent toward Nate, who seemed to be having a typically male reaction to a blatant come-hither. *Oh, for crying out loud.* This was ludi—

She stopped the mental tirade, shocked at not only the vehemence of her thoughts, but also the decidedly jealous tone. What was that about? Yes, she would always be attracted to Nate, but she had no intentions of acting on those feelings. They'd just reached a truce that she needed to build on so that she still had something that looked like a family. So what did it matter that a short skirt and a bit of cleavage turned him into a teenage boy? That was right. It didn't matter. None of her business.

Thoughts firmly on track, she turned her attention from Nate to Dr. Langston.

"First, I want to tell you how sorry I am for your loss," the doctor said, glancing briefly at Hallie, but talking directly to Nate. "David and Janet were beautiful people."

"Thank you," Nate said.

Hallie mumbled her thanks, too.

"Greg wanted me to meet with you because he knows what a difficult situation you're in. He felt my insight could help you with your parent selection as you go through the readoption process."

"Thank you, Dr. Langston," Nate said. "We need all the help we can get."

Hallie almost kicked him.

Amazing, how chatty Nate had suddenly become.

What happened to brooding and silent?

"Please," she said. "Call me Deb. And if it's okay, I prefer to use your first names, too. I find the less formality between us, the better."

Hallie fought back a gag.

"How involved have you been in Ahn's life since the adoption, Nate?"

"I'm afraid not at all," Nate admitted. "I flew home

for Ahn's christening. But I've been out of the country since then."

"And you, Hallie?" Deb asked, looking directly at Hallie for the first time.

It hurt Hallie to admit that before the accident she'd only seen Ahn four times. At the airport when Janet and David first brought her home. At Ahn's christening. The one weekend she had made time in her busy schedule to stay with Janet and Ahn while David was out of town. And at Ahn's second birthday party—the weekend before the accident on May 2. The last time Hallie had seen Janet and David alive.

"My contact with Ahn has been limited," Hallie said, though she couldn't keep from adding, "but if I remember correctly, that was partially due to advice Janet and David received from you." Down went the gauntlet. She was *not* going to let this woman push her around.

"That's true," Deb said, apparently unruffled by the challenge. "During the first two months after the adoption it was important for Ahn to have time alone with Janet and David in order for them to bond as a family. But I apologize if the question sounded more like an accusation. I was only trying to gauge how much time each of you had been able to spend with Ahn."

Now she was trying to make Hallie look like a bitch.

And okay, she *was* being a bitch. But she was an honest bitch.

"And I apologize for being defensive," Hallie said. "But we all have our regrets. And my regret will always be that I didn't spend more time with my sister and Ahn when Janet was alive."

"And how is Ahn?"

Hallie and Nate looked at each other.

It took Hallie a second to realize Nate was waiting for her to answer the question. As if she could. She was no more qualified to answer the question than Nate.

"Since the accident, my stepmother has been staying at Janet and David's and taking care of Ahn. Nate and I are staying there, too," Hallie added quickly. "But... well, under the circumstances..."

"I understand completely," Deb said. "But I'm pleased to hear Ahn isn't being bounced around from one family member to another while you and Nate are trying to recover. It's very important that she stays in her own home where she feels safe. She's too young to understand what's happened, of course, but you should be prepared for drastic mood swings while she's trying to cope with Janet and David's sudden absence from her life."

Hallie nodded that she understood.

And okay, maybe she'd been too quick to judge.

"And is your stepmother going to stay and help you take care of Ahn until you find new parents?"

"No," Hallie said, shuddering at the thought. She loved Roberta. And she was going to make an effort to get along with her better. But Roberta's overbearing personality had always driven Hallie up the wall. "We're beginning interviews for a full-time nanny this week."

Deb looked surprised. "I strongly advise against hiring a nanny."

Hallie sat straighter in her chair. "Excuse me?"

"I strongly disagree with you leaving Ahn's care to a nanny," she repeated. "Ahn is slowly making progress, but she still has a lot to overcome in order to catch up developmentally. Unless you get to know this child, and I'm talking really get to know Ahn's wants, her needs, her temperament and especially her shortcomings, you'll struggle to choose the best parents for her."

The magnitude of what Deb implied momentarily staggered Hallie. She couldn't take care of Ahn on her own. She didn't know the first thing about child rearing, especially with a child who'd experienced a lack of early stimulation and now needed particular attention. Deb couldn't possibly mean that. "So what are you're suggesting? That I quit my job and take care of Ahn, possibly for months, until we find new parents?"

"If at all possible, yes," Deb said, as if that were a completely reasonable request. She looked over at Nate. "And, if possible, you should do the same, Nate. As Ahn's guardians *and* as the two people who will decide her future, both of you need to take full responsibility as Ahn's primary caregivers so you *will* be qualified to make such an important decision."

Nate looked shocked.

Hallie was speechless.

But she already knew what Nate had to be thinking. Of course it was *possible* for both of them to put their careers on hold until Ahn was readopted. Janet and David had made it possible.

But money wasn't the issue here.

The issue for Hallie was becoming a full-time parent. Hallie couldn't even fathom it. A claustrophobic sensation rose in her. Every day spent locked in a house with her only focus a child with limited communication skills? And she couldn't fathom someone as restless as Nate being stuck at Wedge Pond and helping her take care of a baby.

"I appreciate the advice, but we *will* be hiring a nanny," Hallie told her firmly. She reached into her purse and handed over the form Greg had given them. "Greg said you would help us fill this out for the adoption agency."

Dr. Langston took the paper but the look she gave Hallie said she wasn't through. "I'll be happy to help you. And maybe as we go over the parental requirements Ahn will need, you'll reconsider your decision about the nanny."

Don't count on it.

If Janet and David had thought Hallie and Nate were capable of raising their daughter, they wouldn't have assigned their siblings the role of guardian with the task of finding new parents. But Janet and David hadn't and that, to Hallie's way of thinking, was proof enough that she couldn't provide the care Ahn required. So Dr. Langston was *not* going to lay some guilt trip on her sufficient enough to make Hallie embrace a role she knew absolutely zero about. She'd never even been a babysitter as a teenager. Kids had always been Janet's thing, not hers.

Dr. Langston reached for a pen from the holder on her desk. "I don't know how much David and Janet shared with you about how Ahn spent the first eighteen months of her life in the orphanage. There were too many children and not enough staff, so only Ahn's basic needs were met. Human contact was limited to when Ahn was fed or when she was changed. And since babies are immobile, they always get the least attention. Ahn's days were spent alone in a crib, left to entertain herself."

She paused. "That was the bad news. The good news is that there is nothing physically wrong with her. David and Janet have had her to the best pediatric specialists available and she's perfectly healthy. She has a lot of catching up to do developmentally, but she's a very bright child. With the right parental support she'll thrive and she'll be on par with her peers by the time she starts school."

She checked a box on the form. "I'm recommending a stay-at-home parent on this form. Ahn's best chance for overcoming her problems is a parent who can give Ahn the attention she needs. And by attention, I mean the daily verbal, cognitive and physical exercises Ahn has been receiving these past six months."

She opened a desk drawer and pulled out a thick bound notebook that she handed directly to Hallie. "This notebook gives you a concise description of the exercises Janet has been following. Take this copy in case Janet's has been misplaced."

Reluctantly, Hallie took it. The size of the book represented a level of responsibility and dedication she had never given another human being. This was where Janet had excelled. She'd been so compassionate and caring, so willing and able to pull people under her wing and foster them until they were strong enough to stand on their own. With her as a mommy, Hallie had no doubt Ahn would have been a match for any kid in her classes.

But that was Janet's forte, not Hallie's. Hallie organized action and information. She could pull together all the unruly and disparate pieces that her show required and execute it flawlessly. She dealt in the realm of theory and ideas. People? Not so much.

This book seemed to shout all of her inadequacies loud enough for all to hear. She set it on the floor by her purse, thinking she'd read it later when she wasn't feeling so overwhelmed.

"Ahn's daily activities are also why I feel so strongly that one or both of you should fill in as a stay-at-home parent. Since Janet stayed with Ahn, she might connect better with you, Hallie. And while I appreciate that you could hire a female nanny, I fear if Ahn's care is turned over to someone who has no personal interest in her, she will receive little more than what she received at the orphanage. Only her basic needs will be met. That could result in Ahn regressing instead of moving forward. She needs the support of someone who is fully committed to her improvement. What she doesn't need is someone who takes care of her only in order to earn a paycheck."

"Greg mentioned it was possible that Ahn's delayed speech development could make it more difficult to find parents for her," Nate said. "Do you agree?"

"Unfortunately, yes," she said. "But as I mentioned before, Ahn is a very bright child. If you take this opportunity to work closely with her, the speech problem may take care of itself."

She checked another box. "Again, because of Ahn's special needs, there should be no other siblings. The parents need to be able to devote their full attention to Ahn without any other distractions. As she gets older, siblings would actually be a benefit to her."

Deb paused and considered Hallie and Nate. "I've been referring to parents in general so far. It's quite likely you'll want Ahn's prospective parents to mirror what she had—a mother who stays at home and a father who works out of the house. If that's the case, here are some things to look for. The best father for Ahn won't travel, and will be at home at night. All children need a strong male presence, but Ahn needs consistency. A father she sees only on weekends can't provide that. Nor can a workaholic father. Ahn needs a father who is willing to be one hundred percent involved in her overall care. And she needs a father who wants a child because he's ready to be a father, and not because his wife wants to be a mother."

She paused again. "To put it bluntly, more than half

of the adoptive fathers I work with go through the adoption process only to please their wives." She looked at Nate. "I can assure you, your brother wasn't one of them. David was one of the most committed fathers I've ever worked with. Ahn was shy and withdrawn around him at first, but she quickly became attached. In order to lessen the void Ahn feels in her life right now, it would help if you filled in so she still has that strong male presence and will be better able to bond with her new father."

"I'm confused," Hallie said. "How do you expect *us* to determine whether a man is ready to be a father for the right reasons? It isn't likely he's going to admit that to us even if we asked."

"True," Deb said. "Hopefully you'll pick up on any red flags when you meet the applicants face-to-face."

Hallie had no reply—she was too overwhelmed.

Dammit, where had her mind been? Why hadn't she realized before now how hard choosing parents for Ahn was going be? How much was at stake?

Of course, Hallie already knew the answer.

Until now she'd seen her role as a supervisory one, directing other people the way she did on the job. But she'd never envisioned herself doing all the tasks Janet had on a daily basis.

"That takes care of most of the form," Dr. Langston said, checking a few more boxes. "These last four questions are ones the two of you need to answer based on your personal preferences. They have nothing to do with my professional opinion."

She poised her pen over the paper. "Are you open to older parents? Or do you prefer younger parents?"

"Mid- to late-thirties, I guess," Nate said, looking over at Hallie. "The same age as David and Janet?"

"I agree," Hallie said.

"Number of years you feel the couple should be married?"

"At least five years?" Hallie suggested.

Nate nodded.

"The lowest income level you'd consider?"

"No lower than two-fifty a year," Nate said without even asking Hallie. "Otherwise the new parents won't be able to provide Ahn with whatever extra help she needs."

"I agree," Dr. Langston said. "At this point there's no way to tell if Ahn is going to need additional counseling and therapy on a long-term basis."

She looked back down at the form. "Are you open to out-of-state applicants?"

"I'd prefer in-state applicants," Hallie said. "Or at least applicants who live in and around our neighboring northeastern states. I'm retaining my right to stay in touch with Ahn after the adoption. The less distance between us, the easier that will be."

Dr. Langston was bold enough to say, "Really? That surprises me since you're so determined to have a nanny."

"I may not be the mommy type, but Ahn is my niece. The adoption isn't going to change that as far as I'm concerned."

Dr. Langston finished making her notations on the form. "That concludes the questionnaire," she said, handing the form across the desk. "And for what it's worth, I think Ahn is a lucky little girl to have you for an aunt, Hallie."

"Thank you." Hallie stood and stuck out her hand. "And thanks for your help today."

Deb stood and shook Hallie's hand.

Hallie put the form in her purse and stuck the notebook under her arm then followed as Dr. Langston walked them to her office door.

"I've made an appointment for Ahn in two weeks," Deb said. "With the drastic changes going on in her life right now, it's important that you keep the appointment."

"She'll be here," Nate said.

Hallie knew there were questions she should probably ask—behaviors to watch out for, or strategies to deal with Ahn's grief—but her mind was spinning from too much information, and her head was pounding from a stress-induced headache. All Hallie wanted was out of here.

And maybe after a few hours of solitude this insane reality she was living would make sense.

CHAPTER FOUR

NATE HAD NEVER CLAIMED to be a genius. But he was smart enough to stay out of the middle of a disagreement between two strong and independent women. Only a fool would get involved once the claws came out.

So when Deb and Hallie had come down on opposite sides of the nanny debate, he'd kept his mouth shut.

Just as he was keeping his mouth shut now.

Hallie had not said a word when he'd caught up with her at the elevator. Not after she popped two aspirin into her mouth from the bottle she dropped back into her purse. Not when they'd stopped at Greg's office to drop off the information for the adoption agency. Not during the three-block walk to the parking garage. And not when he'd opened the passenger-side door so she could climb into his Range Rover.

They were driving out of downtown Boston now, heading back to Wedge Pond. And Hallie had yet to say a word.

But Nate didn't have to glance over at her sitting in the seat beside him to know she was chewing on her lower lip. He'd seen her do it a thousand times. Hallie always chewed on her lower lip when she was worried about something.

Nate also didn't have to wonder what that something was. Dr. Langston's advice about the nanny had been shocking and eye-opening—for both of them.

The question was what to do about it.

Nate tried to picture him and Hallie taking care of Ahn. He couldn't. His inability to see it had nothing against Hallie and definitely nothing against Ahn. It was him and his decision never to have kids. He didn't have it in him to be daddy to anyone—even on a temporary basis. But instinct told him not to discuss the issue until Hallie was ready.

Nate had no intention of doing or saying anything that might damage the truce he and Hallie had finally found. That ground was still too shaky, too new to both of them.

Besides, they weren't used to talking to each other at all. One conversation in a bathroom wasn't going to instantly change that. They'd have to gradually ease into a comfort zone with each other. He'd give Hallie all the space and all the time she needed until she could begin to feel comfortable around him.

Unfortunately, feeling comfortable around each other could lead to another problem. From what Greg and Deb had told them, finding new parents wasn't going to be easy. And that meant he and Hallie could be spending far more time together than Nate ever imagined.

He was concerned about that.

Gravely concerned.

Nate almost wished he had lied to Hallie when she'd confronted him about their past. That he'd allowed her to keep thinking he was an egotistical bastard. Her disdain toward him had cancelled out his attraction to her all these years, the same as her age had stopped him from acting when they first met.

Only Hallie wasn't a kid anymore.

She was a beautiful, desirable woman who was extremely vulnerable at the moment.

Fate had forced them together at the worst possible time. Losing David and Janet had turned their lives upside down. Thrown them completely off-kilter. Left them both floundering, uncertain what they should do first or which way they should turn next.

An affair right now would only end in disaster. They were both too unstable.

The question was, did he have the same strength he'd had ten years ago? Could he really resist Hallie if they were together day and night? Nate wasn't sure that he could again do what was best for Hallie under the circumstances.

Nate glanced over at her.

He was surprised to see she was staring right at him.

"So?" she said. "What do you think about the nanny situation?"

He wondered if she'd be shocked to know he hadn't been thinking about the nanny situation at all. That he'd been thinking about the things they'd done to each other in the back of that taxi.

"I don't think we have any choice but to hire a nanny. But I can also understand Deb's reasons for why we shouldn't."

"Really?" she said. "I'm amazed you heard a word she said with the amount of cleavage she was showing."

"Is that a hint of meow in your voice?" Nate asked.

"Of course it is," she admitted. "From a woman's point of view, the only thing worse than another woman being so gorgeous is if she's smart and gorgeous."

"If that's true," Nate said, "then I'm sure she was thinking the same thing about you."

She snorted. "Have you looked at me today?"

Much more often than I should have.

But Nate wisely chose not to answer. "Does your question mean you're having second thoughts about the nanny?"

"No," she said. "I'm having terrifying thoughts about not hiring a nanny and taking up the role as Ahn's primary caregiver." She waved the notebook at him. "I don't even have to open this notebook to know how doomed Ahn would be if she had to rely on me to help progress those developmental skills *Deb* kept talking about. I'm not even capable of fulfilling the child's *basic* needs. I don't do diapers."

"I don't do diapers, either. But maybe we could compromise. We could hire a nanny to take care of Ahn's basic needs. And one of us could take responsibility for working with Ahn on a personal level."

"One of us meaning *me*," Hallie said, "since you'll be heading back to Afghanistan."

Nate kept his eyes straight ahead when he said, "I'm not going back to Afghanistan, Hallie. I arranged for my replacement before I left."

She gasped. "But why?"

Nate still didn't look at her. "My mother. With David gone, I need to be able to check on her."

Instantly, Hallie's hand was on his arm.

Instantly, her touch left Nate rattled.

"Oh, God, Nate. I'm sorry. I haven't thought about your mother."

"No need to apologize," Nate said, relieved when she withdrew her hand. But he did glance over at her. "My mother isn't going to realize I'm there, of course. Just like she didn't realize David came to see her every week. But I'll know."

Nate looked back at the highway.

"Do you get that's the same way I feel about Ahn? I need to know I didn't turn my back on her."

"When you put it that way, yes. I do understand how you feel."

"Look at us," she said. "We're actually agreeing on something."

"And I hope you'll agree with something else," Nate told her. "Since I'm not going back to Afghanistan, I should be the one to stay with Ahn and the nanny. That will leave you free to go home and back to work."

Hallie sent him a wary look.

"When you're ready to go back to work, of course," Nate added quickly.

"I never considered you wouldn't go back. But

you're right. The fact that you're staying changes everything."

"I'm not sure what you mean."

"I mean, of course you'll stay at the house, Nate. You live there."

She was referring to the guest cottage on David and Janet's property. It wasn't feasible to maintain a stateside apartment when he was out of the country most of the time, so he'd been using the cottage as his residence.

"Did you really think if I stayed at Janet and David's I would expect you to leave?" she asked.

"Before we had our conversation in the bathroom this morning, yes."

"Well, you're wrong," she said. "Even if we'd never talked, I wouldn't have expected you to leave just because I was staying there."

"And your thoughts on my proposal about the nanny?"

"You can really see yourself being a world-renowned photojournalist turned verbal, cognitive and physical child therapist?"

"No," Nate admitted. "But I also can't see you resigning and putting your career on hold when I'm free to stay with Ahn."

"So I get a pass," she said, "and you get stuck with all the responsibility."

"I prefer to think of it as making a logical decision under the circumstances."

She looked over at him. "I can't go to work and not feel guilty about it."

"Then stay on the weekends if that will make you feel less guilty." That arrangement was still potentially dangerous by putting them in proximity and giving them the opportunity to act on what was going on between them. He wasn't so naive as to think they'd be able to resist—truly only her animosity toward him all these years had accomplished that. But if he could restrict her time in the house to weekends he might be able to forestall them landing in bed.

So he had to convince her to return to work. And he'd figure out how to step into Ahn's daily learning regimen.

Hallie's silence stretched out. When he glanced at her she was rubbing her temples with her fingertips. Was that because she found his suggestion so outrageous she was pissed at him? Or did she think it had merit? He latched on to the fact she hadn't said no yet. He didn't intend to lose his momentum.

"You heard what Deb said about Ahn being more likely to bond with her new father if I stepped in. That's another reason I should be the one to stay."

She let out a long sigh. "And I also heard what she said about me not being able to properly evaluate the applicants if I've never played the parent role." She looked over at him. "Admit it. I'm obviously not a very good judge of character, or I wouldn't have been so wrong about you all these years."

He couldn't let her take responsibility for reacting to a situation he'd created. "That was my fault."

"Truthfully, Nate, I'm not capable of making any decisions right now. Okay?"

"Absolutely." He could commiserate. The only thing that kept him choosing one thing over another these days was experience—once upon a time he'd been in similar circumstances with far fewer resources and less maturity. "Think about it and we'll discuss it later."

As Nate focused on the highway, he was relieved she hadn't immediately shot down his solution to the problem. The fact that they'd had a rational discussion reinforced the rightness of his impulse to tell her the truth about his attraction all those years ago. He'd thought that information would go to the grave with him. But he was glad she knew—she didn't deserve to think less of herself because of his sense of self-preservation.

Sure, he'd have to keep a check on his attraction to her—something that would be much easier if she weren't living at the house. But the most important thing now was for them to be able to look at the situation in a logical manner.

Hopefully Hallie would see his suggestion made the most sense.

Surely, she would realize that.

HALLIE WAS RELIEVED when Nate headed for the guest cottage once they arrived at the house. As strained as it had been not talking to each other for the past few weeks, Hallie found it as difficult now that they were talking.

Or maybe it was only *what* they were talking about.

It would take days to completely wrap her mind around everything that had happened this morning. Her mind-blowing inheritance. Her big showdown with Nate. The reality check she'd gotten about the nanny. Then Nate's suggestion that she return to work and let him take care of Ahn with a nanny's help.

Hallie was too confused to process anything, her mind jammed with information overload.

As she walked to the main house, her thoughts travelled back four years to when she, Janet and David had driven out here to Winchester, an upscale little town north of Boston. Once Janet and David made the decision to adopt, they'd started house hunting immediately. Winchester had been at the top of their short list because it was one hundred percent family-focused.

Hallie hadn't been surprised when Janet instantly fell in love with this two-story contemporary, all stone and glass, that was situated on three acres of waterfront property facing Wedge Pond. The house had Janet's name written all over it. But Hallie knew the guest cottage adjacent to the main house was what had sold David on the place.

She'd been invited to dinner shortly after Janet and David moved in, as had Nate, home for a quick stay between assignments. It was one of the few times she hadn't dragged a date along. Hallie would never forget the proud look on David's face when he'd handed Nate the keys to the cottage.

"Welcome home, brother," David had said. "Your keys. Your cottage. My thanks for all you've done for me."

Because of their mother's chronic depression, David had always given Nate credit for making sure he had a home when they were growing up. The cottage finally provided David with a way to pay Nate back.

Now, David and Janet had left the property to both of them. But as far as Hallie was concerned, the place belonged to Nate. After the readoption, she would sign over her half and give it to Nate free and clear.

And she wasn't going to argue with Nate about it.

She had no use for a rambling two-story house. Especially not out in the suburbs. She was a city girl through and through, and she loved her downtown Boston apartment.

It made her wonder if Nate had any idea how tempting his offer was. She would give anything to go home. To sleep in her own bed. To try to re-create some normalcy in her life.

As if her life ever would be normal again.

Hallie took a deep breath and started up the steps that led to the back deck overlooking Wedge Pond. The French doors off the den had always been the entryway everyone used into the house.

With any luck, Roberta would be in the kitchen, too busy with Ahn to pay much attention when Hallie snuck upstairs to lie down. Words like *tired, stressed* or *headache* were a sign of weakness to Roberta. She expected everyone to do as she did—suck it up and move on. After hearing every excuse possible during her forty years of teaching, Roberta had zero tolerance for excuses and held the opinion that whining shouldn't be tolerated.

Hallie's late father and Janet had always done exactly what Roberta wanted in order to keep the peace. Hallie had been the only one who ever stood up to her—the main reason they had trouble getting along.

After the morning she'd had, Hallie knew a run-in with Roberta might really push her over the edge. She was tired. She was stressed. And yes, she had a monster of a headache.

Unfortunately, when Hallie reached the top step, there sat Roberta, a book on her lap, the baby monitor on the table beside her.

Hallie walked in her direction.

A glance at the video screen on the monitor showed Ahn was sleeping peacefully in her crib. Roberta's expression, however, was anything but peaceful. The strain of the tragedy still showed plainly on her face.

For the first time ever Hallie thought she looked old.

Old was not an adjective anyone used to describe Roberta Weston. At sixty-seven, she was still trim, still full of energy, and she could have easily passed for fifty-seven if she covered up the gray at her temples, which she absolutely refused to do.

"God gives you gray hair for a reason," she always declared. "It reminds you to be thankful for every day you have left on this Earth."

But Hallie couldn't think about God right now. She was much too angry.

Roberta closed her book and placed it on the table by the monitor as Hallie approached. She flopped into the adjacent deck chair, set down her purse and the notebook, then kicked off her high heels.

"Don't get too comfortable. I made tuna salad for lunch. You need to eat something."

"Thanks," Hallie said. "But I'll eat later."

"You always say that," Roberta countered. "But you never follow through."

Hallie refused to argue. Wasn't that her goal? To try to get along better?

"Starving yourself doesn't solve anything, Hallie."

Teetering close to the edge, Hallie said, "I'm not starving myself. I just don't have an appetite."

"Then either force yourself to eat, or get a new wardrobe," Roberta said. "That dress looks awful on you."

What could Hallie say to that? It was true.

So rather than fight Hallie changed the subject. "Greg's going to call you this afternoon."

Roberta's head jerked in her direction. "Me?"

"Janet and David named you in the will," Hallie said. "Greg said they left you a monetary gift and he wants to discuss it with you."

Roberta pursed her lips. "There was absolutely no reason for Janet and David to do that. I'm hardly destitute."

After Hallie's father died five years ago, Roberta retired from teaching, sold the house and bought a condo in a retirement community for active seniors. She played tennis twice a week, worked out in the gym every morning, in addition to her busy social life. And recently, she'd met a retired Air Force colonel who lived in the same complex. The Colonel, as Roberta fondly called him, had come to the funeral to lend his support—support Roberta was going to need in the long, hard days that still lay ahead.

"I know you aren't destitute, Roberta," Hallie said patiently. "And Janet and David knew it, too. But they loved you." Hallie stole Greg's line. "Accept their gift in the spirit it was given."

That silenced Roberta.

Was Roberta hard to get along with? Yes. Was her personality abrasive? Definitely. But there was no doubt in Hallie's mind that Roberta had always cared about her and Janet. She was always there for direction and for guidance—just not so much on an emotional level. She'd basically treated her stepdaughters the same way she'd treated her students. And while there was nothing wrong with that, secretly Hallie would have preferred a little less practical logic and a little more loving compassion.

"The nanny agency called to confirm your first interview appointment tomorrow," Roberta said.

If Hallie heard the word *nanny* one more time today, she was going to scream. "Good. I can never thank you enough for taking care of Ahn these past three weeks, Roberta. But I know you're ready to go home."

Roberta didn't deny it. "There's no need to thank me

for anything. That's what families do in a crisis. They step in and do what needs to be done."

With Deb's dire warning echoing in her head, Hallie sought another opinion. "So you agree, then? Hiring a nanny is our best choice?"

"Of course I agree," Roberta said. "Who would take care of Ahn if you didn't hire a nanny? You?" Roberta had the nerve to laugh.

Hallie bristled, even though she felt the same way. "That's what Ahn's psychologist thinks we should do. She advises against hiring a nanny. She thinks Nate and I should be Ahn's primary caregivers until the readoption so we will be able to choose the best parents for her."

"And how is Nate supposed to do that from Afghanistan?" Her tone clearly said what she thought of the doctor's recommendation.

"Nate isn't going back. He's staying here. Someone has to be available to check on his mother."

"And what are you supposed to do? Take Ahn to work with you?"

Hallie sighed. "No. I'd have to ask for an indefinite leave of absence. Or turn in my resignation if they refuse to give me one."

"That's ridiculous," Roberta said. "You can't be expected to quit your job. And what kind of idiot would suggest that two people who have no experience taking care of a baby, let alone one who needs special attention, should act as the child's primary caregivers?"

"Nate and I aren't imbeciles, Roberta. We could learn to take care of a baby."

Roberta shook her head in disgust. "Well, as far as I'm concerned, this doctor is the imbecile. That's why I've never had any faith in psychologists. They're all idealistic snobs completely out of touch with reality."

Her words should have made Hallie feel better. Too bad they didn't.

Hallie grabbed the notebook and held it up for Roberta to see. "Have you been following Janet's copy of Ahn's daily developmental exercises?"

Roberta straightened into her stern no-nonsense teacher pose. "Absolutely not. I told Janet from the beginning what I thought about that hogwash. Parents today rely too much on so-called experts to tell them how to raise their children, without realizing that within five years the opinion will change, and everything they've been doing is now considered wrong. Parents know best what's right for their children."

There was truth in what Roberta said. But still Hallie was worried. Ahn's situation was different. She'd been cheated out of a normal start in life. She hadn't had parents in the beginning, following some expert's guidelines or otherwise.

Roberta started to say something else but a slight noise from the monitor stopped her.

Hallie leaned past Roberta to look at the screen. Ahn was now sitting up in her crib. She wasn't making any effort to get out nor was she making a sound. She remained in place, her thumb in her mouth, patiently waiting until someone noticed she was awake.

Roberta stood. "Time for a diaper change, then lunch."

Basic needs, Hallie thought.

"Wait." Hallie rose. "I'll go with you. I think it's time I learned to change a diaper."

"You? Change a diaper?"

"Are you still a good teacher? Or have you lost your touch?" Hallie challenged.

Without a word Roberta led the way into the house. Hallie followed, notebook in hand. She'd told Nate earlier she wasn't capable of making any decisions right now.

Obviously, she'd lied.

CHAPTER FIVE

HALLIE HAD CHANGED her first diaper.

Well, sort of. She'd started the process with Ahn lying on the changing table and Roberta looking over her shoulder telling her what to do. But the second Hallie actually saw—and smelled—the contents of the diaper, she'd made a mad dash for the bathroom down the hall from the nursery with her hand over her mouth.

Hallie still felt a little nauseous as she walked back into the nursery. Thankfully, Roberta had taken care of the problem. The mess was gone and Ahn awaited a fresh diaper.

"Sorry," Hallie said, looking at Ahn. "Aunt Hallie has a weak stomach."

Ahn didn't look at her.

Why would Hallie expect anything else? This was the first time she'd ever interacted with Ahn personally. She'd always been in the background looking on—an observer, not a caregiver.

She hadn't even been a good observer, not really.

Sure, she knew Janet was concerned about Ahn's delayed speech and her other developmental problems. But Janet had been concerned about everything involving Ahn. Hallie had put those concerns down to new mommy syndrome.

If only she'd paid more attention. If only she'd been there for Janet. If only she'd been a concerned sister and a concerned aunt.

"The insert goes into the slot on her diaper panty," Roberta instructed.

Hallie placed an eco-friendly insert into the slot of Ahn's pink reusable diaper panty as Roberta instructed, thinking the whole eco-thing was *so* Janet and David. They had been organic about everything. But her diet wasn't the only aspect of Ahn's life that had been carefully structured and monitored. There were the play groups with scheduled dates. And toddler music classes. And a million other progressive-parent babyisms that Hallie knew from listening to Janet rattle on for hours were part of the whole stay-at-home-mom regimen.

Could she really live that kind of lifestyle? Even temporarily?

"Well? What are you waiting for?" Roberta's impatient question broke Hallie's train of thought. And from the expression on her face Roberta was convinced Hallie couldn't handle the demanding job of caring for Ahn.

"Pick the child up," Roberta said. "Take her downstairs so you can fix her lunch."

Hallie picked up Ahn, but she handed her to Roberta when Ahn went rigid in her arms. "I think I'd rather take one thing at a time." Yeah, she hated that she was confirming Roberta's worst opinion but it seemed easier to forestall a tantrum from Ahn than to go out of her way to prove Roberta wrong. Seemed both Hallie and Ahn needed to ease into this relationship.

"That's too bad." Roberta bent to place Ahn on the floor with a toy. When she straightened, she said, "Time is something you don't have. I'm past ready to go home. And I'm too old to be taking care of a baby. I just don't have the energy. I'll stay the rest of this week and give you a crash course on how to take care of her. That's my offer. Take it or leave it."

Hallie stared at her.

"What?" Roberta said. "You think I didn't know the minute you decided to change a diaper that you had also decided to take that quack psychologist's advice? My question is, how are you and Nate going to survive playing house without killing each other?"

Roberta wanted details? Hallie would give her details.

"Nate and I had a long talk this morning," Hallie admitted. "We cleared the air between us. And we *won't* be playing house. Nate will be living in the cottage the same way he always has. And I'll be living here in the house with Ahn." And where had that decision come from? Especially without consulting Nate first? Was this her typical knee-jerk reaction to Roberta's domination? While that factored, Hallie had to admit there was something more to this sudden change of heart. Ahn deserved more than Hallie had given her so far and this was her chance to do better.

"If you believe that arrangement will last," Roberta

said, "then you'll believe I'm going to use Janet and David's *monetary gift* to get a boob job."

Hallie's mouth dropped open.

"Oh, please," Roberta said. "Do you really think it's been a secret that you and Nate had a fling back in the day and that you've been mad at him all these years because he dumped you?"

Hallie's mouth closed. "Whatever happened between us back in the day is over. And I intend for it to stay that way."

Roberta laughed. "That's the signal you think you're sending Nate by quitting your job so the two of you can play mommy and daddy? I don't think so."

Hallie wasn't only over the edge, she was the splat at the bottom of the cliff.

"I don't want to talk about this any further, Roberta. I'm serious. I'm going to go lie down now and sleep off this headache. And yes, I am going to take you up on your offer to stay the rest of the week and show me how to take care of Ahn. I'll sincerely appreciate it if you'll do that. But whatever happened between Nate and I, or whatever might happen between us in the future, frankly is none of your business."

Hallie pushed past her out of the nursery.

"What are you going to do when you have a headache while you're taking care of Ahn?" Roberta called after her. "You won't be able to lie down and sleep it off then."

"I'll suck it up and deal." Hallie headed for Janet and

David's bedroom, where she'd been staying since the accident.

Slamming the bedroom door definitely didn't help the headache. But climbing onto Janet and David's big four-poster bed, pulling the covers over her head and closing her eyes did.

At least two hours mental shutdown time. That was all she needed.

And when she got up, Hallie *was* going to suck it up and deal. She was going to take charge of the situation the same way she took charge at the station every day.

It had taken Roberta's indifference to Ahn's special needs to make Hallie realize she'd made the same mistake. She'd assumed all Ahn needed was a nanny to take care of her basic needs until they found new parents.

But Hallie couldn't lie to herself anymore.

If she were going to be the type of aunt she wanted to be, she had to put Ahn's needs above her own. And whether she was emotionally ready or not, she had no choice.

NATE STEPPED OUT of the shower and dried himself off, hoping Hallie had spent the afternoon thinking over their circumstances so they could talk about it after dinner tonight. The evening meal was the only one Nate ate at the main house and he did that because he knew if he didn't, Roberta would be insulted. When she cooked, she expected people to eat. She was a hard woman to stand up to.

Now that he and Hallie were on speaking terms,

Nate was relieved his plan to have a talk with Roberta wouldn't be necessary. He never quite knew what to expect from her. She could be nice and friendly one minute, then could shred a person to pieces the next. As a result, he did his best to stay on Roberta's good side.

Nate checked his watch. It was only 5:45 and Roberta served dinner promptly at six—being late wasn't an option.

Nate walked out of the bathroom, grabbed the clean boxers he'd placed on the bed and stepped into them. Jeans and a T-shirt would have been his preference, but Roberta insisted everyone dress for dinner.

He slid his arms into the sleeves of a dress shirt, and pulled on a pair of pants. As he looked around for his shoes, Nate thought of how Janet had also preferred dressing for dinner. Made sense. She had, after all, grown up with that tradition.

Instead of being commanding like Roberta, and jerking the plates right out from under you the minute you finished eating, Janet had been the nurturing type. You could tell Janet enjoyed making the evening meal special, eating in the dining room, putting out the good china, serving after-dinner coffee and encouraging everyone to linger for after-dinner conversation.

Not once had Nate sat at Janet's table and not been thankful she was David's wife. After David met Janet, everything his brother had always wanted seemed to click into place. He had a beautiful wife who loved him. A beautiful home. They'd finally adopted the child they'd always wanted.

Deb Langston didn't have to tell Nate what a committed father David was. David's entire life had revolved around Janet and Ahn. They were the center of his world. His reason for existing.

All the things Nate didn't want. He'd learned a long time ago that what you wanted most was what life didn't let you keep.

Weren't David and Janet proof of that?

They'd had everything they wanted most, then a drunk driver had taken their lives in the blink of an eye. As cynical and coldhearted and as guilty as Nate felt about the thought, he was still glad David and Janet died together.

Neither of them would have survived without the other.

Just like his mother hadn't been able to survive without his dad.

That was why he lived in the moment. No personal attachments. And no promises life wouldn't let him keep.

Too bad his own convictions didn't excuse him from the promises other people made, however. And too bad that even though he'd been successful in shutting down his heart, he'd been less successful in turning off his conscience.

In truth, Nate's conscience was all he had left.

That was why he was fully committed to making sure Ahn did have the type of future David and Janet had promised to give her. Whatever it took, Nate intended to make that happen.

As he entered the main room of the cottage, socks in hand, still looking for his shoes, a knock at the door jerked his head around. Nate's first thought was that something was wrong. Hallie and Roberta never came down to the cottage. They always used the intercom that connected the cottage to the house if they wanted to communicate with him.

Nate tossed the socks onto the sofa and, his shirt still unbuttoned, hurried to open the door. Hallie was on the other side.

But not the unkempt and frazzled Hallie he'd been seeing for the past three weeks. Her hair was clean and shiny, her makeup was on and the off-the-shoulder green sweater she wore was just revealing enough to take Nate's thoughts to the night she had taken her shirt off on the dance floor.

"I thought we'd eat alone tonight," she said. "So we could talk in private."

Nate looked down at the tray she was holding.

There were two covered plates along with silverware wrapped in linen napkins, wineglasses turned upside down and one bottle of red wine already uncorked. All the requisite pieces for a dinner for two. Alone. Just the two of them.

Damn. He really didn't want alone time with her.

"Is that a problem?" she asked when he didn't respond.

"No. Of course not," Nate said, stepping aside.

She walked past him heading for the banquette built into the kitchen's breakfast nook. Nate's gaze fell to the back of her jeans—a little loose from the weight she'd lost but not loose enough to keep his pulse from kicking up a notch. Yep. This could go very wrong.

She looked over her shoulder as she placed the tray on the table. "Go put on something comfortable. I'm not Roberta. You don't have to dress for dinner with me."

Nate obeyed, partly because he needed a minute to put together his game plan. No matter what his libido wanted there would be no seduction tonight. He'd listen to her, answer appropriately and hold on to whatever gruesome images necessary to keep from picturing the two of them getting tangled in the sheets.

Belatedly he registered her words. She wanted to talk in private, making Nate wonder what they had to talk about that was so private. It wasn't as if Roberta didn't know everything about the situation they were in.

Not another rendition of what had happened ten years ago, he hoped. Hopefully, they'd put that issue to rest forever. But you never knew with women. Sometimes women had to talk an issue to death before they could move on.

Nate groaned at that thought.

He walked to the dresser in his bedroom and grabbed a T-shirt from the drawer, then took a pair of jeans from the drawer directly below it.

Or, Nate decided as he changed clothes, maybe Hallie had spent the afternoon thinking over his proposal. Maybe she'd decided that she would go back to work. That would certainly explain the sudden transformation—in her appearance and in her attitude.

She seemed more confident. Not so rattled and on edge. And she didn't look as if she were ready to cry at any minute. By the time he finished changing Nate had convinced himself that whatever Hallie had to tell him was good news. Why else would she show up unexpectedly with food and wine?

HALLIE HAD ARRANGED everything while Nate changed. She'd even poured the wine. But Nate's comfort had little to do with why she'd told him to go change.

Her own comfort was her concern.

She'd almost dropped the tray when he'd opened the door, his shirt unbuttoned, his tanned six-pack abs staring her in the face. Unfortunately, it wasn't until Nate emerged from the bedroom that Hallie realized asking him to change was a big mistake.

He would have eventually buttoned his shirt. But the black T-shirt he now wore hugged every muscle. And he looked so good in his faded jeans Hallie took a long swallow from her wineglass to hide her gulp.

He slid onto the bench seat across from her.

"Roberta's lasagna," he said, examining his plate. He looked at her and smiled. "My favorite."

She waited until he'd taken a few bites of lasagna and even waited until he'd enjoyed a few sips of wine, before diving into their discussion.

"I want you to hear me out before you say a word. Agreed?" She knew extracting the promise was probably the fastest way for him to put his guard up, but she needed him to listen to her rationale before jumping in to tell her why it wouldn't work.

He nodded, but he reached for his wineglass again.

"Everything Dr. Langston said this morning pissed me off. I didn't want to hear it. I wanted to hold on to my righteous indignation that she would expect me to quit my job and put my career on hold when an experienced nanny could take far better care of Ahn than I could."

Hallie leaned back. "Then you offered me the perfect solution. And God, you have no idea how much I want to take you up on that offer. But I can't."

Nate started to say something.

Hallie held her hand up to stop him.

"So," she said. "Now I'm going to propose something to you. And surprisingly, it's the exact thing Dr. Langston said we should do. We forget the nanny, and we both take care of Ahn. Could you agree to that?"

ALL THE REASONS not to agree flooded Nate's mind.

Sadly they had very little to do with Ahn and everything to do with him and Hallie ending up in bed.

He wanted Hallie desperately. Sitting across from her now he wanted her as much as he had ten years ago. And with the misunderstanding of the past cleared up, his desire for her had been given a green light. But if they slept together, then what? A brief affair was all Nate had ever had to offer her—he didn't do commitment. So they'd have their fun and what if they crashed and burned before finding suitable parents for Ahn? How could a return to hostility between him and Hallie benefit Ahn if they were joint caregivers? Sure, if he was a better man, he'd keep his urges to himself. But he was honest enough to admit he didn't have it in him to resist an agreeable, let's-get-along Hallie.

She was waiting for his answer. "You're worried we'll end up in bed."

Nate didn't lie. "Yes. Aren't you?"

"Of course I am. We're sitting here now, discussing the most serious decision we've had to make in our lives, and all I can think about is that we're only steps away from the bedroom."

That was a match to his libido. "Don't say things like that."

"You think it's better to pretend that I don't know what you're thinking, and that you don't know what I'm thinking? You think maybe it'll go away?"

"Yes. No." He paused. "Hell, Hallie, I don't know, okay? All I do know is this isn't the right time to have an affair. For either of us."

"Just like ten years ago wasn't the right time?"

She was trying to piss him off. It worked.

"Yeah," Nate said. "Just like ten years ago."

She shrugged. "Okay. We've established the fact that this the wrong time for an affair. But you still haven't answered my question. Are you willing to help me take care of Ahn?"

This is why women should come with a warning label. Blows hot one minute, ice-cold the next.

"I'm not sure we're capable of taking care of Ahn without a nanny."

"Roberta's agreed to stay the rest of the week and show me what I need to know," she said. "But I know my limitations. My cooking sucks. I hate doing laundry. And the thought of trying to keep a two-story house clean makes me want to put a gun to my head. We won't need a nanny if you help me take care of Ahn. But I do want to hire a housekeeper. Just during the week. I can manage on weekends."

Since he wasn't into domestic duty any more than she was, that made sense. "And you really think we can do this?"

She smiled. "Take care of Ahn? Or stay out of bed?"

"Both," Nate said.

Her expression turned serious. "Yes, Nate. We can do both. We have to do this for Ahn. And we can't risk the fallout of an affair gone bad. We don't have anyone but each other to rely on. And I don't want to lose that."

"I agree," Nate said. Could he do this—care for Ahn and ignore any lustful thoughts Hallie might inspire? It would be a test. But maybe if they kept a buffer between them and Hallie didn't turn on the charm, he could. He owed it to David to try. "Count me in then."

"Thank you," she said. "We're doing the right thing."

Nate expected her to finish eating with him but she slid from the booth and headed for the door. Nate didn't try to stop her and Hallie didn't look back as she closed the door behind her.

He knew what she was thinking.

She knew what he was thinking.

And they both knew what they were thinking would never simply go away.

CHAPTER SIX

IF HALLIE HAD KNOWN how hard Roberta's crash course in child care was going to be, she would have taken Nate's offer and run to the TV studio without a backward glance. Nothing seemed as arduous as baby boot camp with Roberta as the drill sergeant. But by the end of the week, Hallie had semimastered the changing, the feeding and the bathing. The damn hair-fixing still gave her a fit.

Hallie had always worn her curly hair short so all she had to do was blow her hair dry and let it fall where it wanted. Janet had always complained about that. Just as she'd always complained that Hallie got their mother's dark hair and olive complexion, while Janet was cursed with the red hair, fair skin and the pale eyebrows and lashes of the Weston side of the family.

"Look at you," Janet would say. "All you have to do is run a comb through your hair and dab on some lip gloss and you look like a fashion model. If I didn't love you so much, I would hate you for that."

Lucky for Hallie, Janet had loved her unconditionally.

Just as Janet had loved the child Hallie was grooming

now, almost ready to go downstairs for breakfast. *If,* that was, Hallie could ever get the blasted ponytail thingy fastened around Ahn's extra fine long, black hair.

"Sorry," Hallie told Ahn for the tenth time.

She had the pigtail on the right side secured. But the one on the left was having none of it.

"Maybe we should just leave one side up and one side down," Hallie said, watching Ahn for her reaction. "Wouldn't Roberta just *love* that."

As usual, Ahn's reaction was the same: blank stare, no response.

Finally, the ponytail holder stayed. "Yay," Hallie said, making direct eye contact with Ahn again. "Say good job, Aunt Hallie. You finally did it."

Ahn, of course, said none of that.

Hallie picked her up and hugged her anyway.

"Ready for breakfast?" Hallie chirped as she carried Ahn toward the stairs. "Can you say breakfast?"

Over the past week, Hallie had studied Deb's notebook until she had it memorized page by page. Hallie was determined to follow what Roberta called hogwash to the letter.

Hallie now knew how important it was to maintain direct eye contact with Ahn when talking to her. And how she needed to talk to her as much as possible to encourage her to repeat the words she heard.

She knew to always applaud and praise Ahn for even the simplest things she tried to do for herself. Which, sadly, Hallie had learned were very few.

She knew that Ahn needed to be held, hugged, kissed

and cuddled as much as possible to help her overcome being so withdrawn and detached. She knew Ahn needed at least one hour of outside playtime every day to get her over her fear of being outdoors. And that Ahn needed to be read to at least once a day, not only as a bonding opportunity, but to stimulate Ahn's cognitive skills by associating pictures with words.

The most challenging thing for Hallie, however, had been the stretching exercises that needed to be performed three times a day so her arm and leg muscles— underdeveloped from being confined to a crib—would continue to strengthen. Ahn hated those exercises. She would jerk away from Hallie when they hurt, but not once had she cried. She'd only look away with that same distant expression.

"Say good morning, Roberta," Hallie instructed when they reached the kitchen. She placed Ahn into her high chair.

"Her pasta is ready," Roberta said.

Hallie walked over and picked up the bowl containing the one thing Ahn would eat without a fight. And by herself. Was mac and cheese a normal breakfast food? No. But getting her to eat was an ongoing battle. Her mainstay at the orphanage had been a bottle. According to the pediatrician, if she would eat pasta, they were to let her have pasta whenever she wanted.

Hallie placed the bowl on the chair tray and pushed it closer to her. Ahn picked up a shell and popped it into her mouth.

"What a smart girl," Hallie said.

"You should be teaching her to eat with her spoon," Roberta commented. "She has a spoon right there. If you don't make her use it, she never will."

"She'll get there," Hallie said. "The important thing right now is that she's eating and that she's feeding herself—even with her fingers."

Roberta snorted. "Says the sudden child expert."

Hallie ignored that comment.

They were both watching Ahn when she suddenly picked up her bowl and placed it upside down on top of her head. Roberta gasped. Hallie clapped her hands.

Finally, a reaction other than a blank stare. Finally, she'd done something a normal kid would do.

"Don't encourage that kind of behavior," Roberta scolded. "She'll only repeat it."

Roberta took the bowl off Ahn's head and began picking gooey pieces of pasta from her hair. Hallie stood back and let her. *Gooey* was right up there with *poopy* in Hallie's book. Ew.

When Roberta finished the task, she looked over at Hallie with a satisfied smile. "Your turn," she said. "She just messed her diaper."

Hallie's stomach rolled over.

But she took a deep breath and held it, grabbed Ahn out of her high chair and headed for the laundry room that served as the downstairs change area. After placing Ahn on the counter, Hallie took another deep breath and commenced with the necessary—and expedient—diaper switch.

"You need to start thinking about potty training,"

Roberta called from the kitchen. "Maybe you can pick up some tips from the women in Janet's play group. Did you ever call Janet's friend Liz back like I told you to?"

"No," Hallie replied, "but I will."

"See that you do. It's rude not to respond to an invitation."

As if Hallie didn't know that.

Roberta was definitely trying to push Hallie's buttons this morning. Roberta knew attending a play group held as much appeal for Hallie as having a root canal. Thank God she was leaving today. Hallie would miss the extra set of hands, but she wouldn't the provocative commentary.

"I hope this housekeeper you've hired doesn't rob you blind," Roberta said when Hallie returned to the kitchen and placed Ahn in her high chair. "It doesn't pay to trust too easily, you know. I'd keep a close eye on her."

"Mrs. Wilson comes with excellent references," Hallie said. "I checked every one of them personally." The woman was Roberta's age, for God's sake. Highly doubtful she was a thief.

Hallie fixed Ahn a second bowl of pasta, then placed it in front of Ahn. She immediately reached out and popped a piece in her mouth.

"Of course, Janet was so efficient and organized she didn't need a housekeeper," Roberta said. "She always planned her days right down to the most minute detail and kept everything under control."

Meaning that Hallie had neither of those skills. It simply wasn't true. She couldn't hold down the job she had without being organized and efficient. But there was no reason to point out that she and Janet had simply focused their skills in separate areas. Roberta had always praised Janet over her—that habit was unlikely to change because Janet wasn't here.

A cold shiver ran straight through Hallie as the details of that fateful day replayed in her mind. How, after dropping off Ahn at her play date, David and Janet had driven separately to the Mercedes dealership to drop off her car for regular maintenance. And it was on their way back to the house together that David's BMW was hit head-on by a drunk driver. Any other day Ahn would have been with them—a sobering thought.

Hallie's heart warmed now when she looked over at Ahn. As long as she had this little girl in her life she would still have a bit of Janet and David in her life, too.

"Well," Roberta said. "I've cooked all week, and I've left you every kind of casserole imaginable in the freezer in case you don't care for the new housekeeper's cooking."

"You don't know how much I appreciate you doing that, Roberta. It will keep me from having to cook on the weekends."

"You're going to have your hands full, there's no doubt about that."

They both glanced at Ahn, who was playing with

her pasta again. The action was Hallie's hint that Ahn was full.

"One more thing."

There was always one more thing with Roberta, but she sounded so serious, Hallie paid attention.

"I know we have our differences, Hallie. And I know I've always been harder on you than I was on Janet. But I've worried about you more. You give off this impression that you don't need anyone but yourself, and we both know that's a lie. Be careful and don't get too attached to Ahn or to Nate. If you do, you'll only end up hurt when you do find new parents."

Hallie didn't know what to say.

So she did the unthinkable. Hallie put her arms around Roberta and hugged her.

Surprisingly, Roberta hugged her back.

"You don't have to worry about me," Hallie said when she stepped out of their embrace. "I'll be careful."

"See that you do." Roberta's tone was back to its usual authoritative note. She looked at her watch. "It's nine o'clock so I guess I'll call Nate on the intercom and let him know I'm ready. You know what traffic in downtown Boston is like. It'll take him at least two hours round trip to my condominium. There's no need to tie up his entire Saturday waiting around on me."

Hallie was surprised when Roberta made the first move this time and reached out and squeezed Hallie's hand. "Just remember, I'm always only a phone call away."

"Same here," Hallie told her. "Always."

NATE HAD REMAINED in the background during Roberta's last week—Hallie's idea, not his. She'd explained that Roberta was not pleased with the idea of them practically living together.

Nate wasn't exactly thrilled about it, either. He wisely didn't point that out to Hallie, however.

The less friction between them, the better.

The less *anything* between them, the better.

The excuse he gave Roberta for staying out of their way had actually been the truth. He'd recently been approached by Dirk Gentry, a filmmaker who wanted to collaborate on a documentary covering the first decade of the new millennium. For many of the headline news events over the past ten years, Nate had been there. And he had more than one award-winning photo to prove it. Dirk had earned a good reputation in documentary filmmaking already. He'd insisted together they would make an unstoppable team. And now that he was on board, Nate hoped Dirk's prediction was as good as his filmmaking.

Earlier, he'd put Dirk off because of his assignment in Afghanistan, not to mention the time it would take to go through his catalog of photos and his film footage. But now that his evenings were free, Nate could devote the time the project required.

When he'd told Hallie about the documentary, she'd seemed as relieved as he was that he had something to occupy his night. As stupid as it sounded, the fact that Hallie did seem relieved actually hurt Nate's ego a little.

Maybe men should also come with a warning label. Not good at dealing with emotions. Ever.

He certainly didn't like dealing with his emotions. Probably the reason he felt the most comfortable hanging out behind the lens of the camera. He liked the distance it gave him, liked that he was part of events without having to personally engage. No surprise then that Hallie's indifference toward him in the past had provided him that same opportunity—to watch her from a safe distance.

Now, however, he had no choice but to interact with Hallie. Was this changed dynamic what had him so confused? He panicked when she plainly let him know she wanted him. Yet he panicked when it appeared that she didn't.

Nate shook his head, his mind too boggled to figure it out. Better to focus on sorting his catalogs and not over-analyze this. He had just picked up another photo album to go through when he heard the intercom click.

"Nate? I'm ready to go now."

He rose and walked over to the box on the wall. "I'll be there in a minute, Roberta."

He wasn't looking forward to the ride. Roberta was a lot like Hallie when it came to saying what was on her mind. He'd already prepared himself to get an earful.

As he approached his SUV where it was parked in the driveway, he found Roberta already seated inside and Hallie standing at the passenger door holding Ahn. The look Hallie shot him seemed to say, "Can't you move any faster?"

He felt like asking her if she wanted to trade places.

Hallie helped Ahn wave goodbye as he reversed out of the driveway. They hadn't even reached the main road when Roberta said, "I don't want Hallie hurt, Nate. There's no use in pretending you don't know what I'm talking about."

"I have no intention of doing anything but helping Hallie take care of Ahn, Roberta."

"Good," she said. "Because you aren't a forever kind of guy, are you, Nate?"

Nate kept his eyes straight ahead. "No. I'm not."

"And you understand you have to leave Hallie alone."

"Yes," Nate said. "I know that."

"Good," Roberta said again. "Hallie is going to need your help. She thinks she's prepared because she made it through this week, but she isn't. Taking care of a toddler is a never-ending responsibility that Hallie isn't expecting."

"I understand," Nate said. "I plan to do my part."

"She's in love with you, you know."

Nate laughed and, this time, he did look over at her. "Now that's where you're wrong, Roberta. Hallie's hated me for years."

"Hated you? Or hated what you did to her?"

I was crazy about you. Hallie's confession flashed through Nate's mind, leaving a twinge of panic in its wake.

"This is going to come as a surprise, but Hallie and I

have already talked about the situation. We both agree Ahn is our top priority. She's all we're interested in. Nothing more."

"I'm glad to hear that," Roberta said. "Hallie needs a friend right now, not a lover. And you're going to need Hallie's friendship, too, even though I suspect that's hard for you to admit."

Nate didn't try to argue with her.

Everything she was saying now was true.

"I know how much you loved your brother and I know how much you're going to miss him," she said. "And I also know what you went through trying to raise him. You did a fine job of that, Nate."

He didn't like dragging up the memories of how hard it had been living with a mother who was so depressed she stayed in bed for weeks at a time. Of how he'd gone from a boy to a man overnight after his father's death. How he'd learned to cook and clean and take over every facet of his younger brother's care as well as his own.

His childhood had been painful for him, and Nate had spent his adulthood trying to forget it.

They rode in silence after that. A long, painful silence. He'd let Roberta have her say—respected her too much to do any differently. But there wasn't much left for them to talk about.

Roberta was a hard woman to like because of her abrasive way of speaking her mind and the high standards she held people to. But she was a good woman to have in your corner—she'd defend one of her own to the ends of the earth. Nate only hoped Hallie realized how lucky she was to have Roberta. He would have given anything if he'd had a mother who'd been so protective of him.

Finally, Nate pulled up in front of Roberta's complex. He was as relieved as Roberta seemed surprised to find The Colonel sitting on a bench outside, patiently awaiting their arrival.

Even though the man was in his seventies, Nate would have pegged him as military at a single glance. The Colonel's gray hair was clipped short, his shirt starched, the crease pressed into his pants razor-sharp. He stood up as Nate came to a stop, shoulders back, head held high, ready to take command of the situation.

Nate got out and walked to the rear of the SUV for Roberta's luggage. The Colonel's handshake was firm and strong. Roberta was so flattered over her new beau fawning over her, Nate was saved from any parting schoolteacher lectures. But her final reply was enough.

'I'll be checking in on things," she said.

Nate knew it wasn't an idle threat and she was referring to more than Ahn's care.

As he headed back to Wedge Pond, everything Roberta had said reverberated through Nate's mind. Regardless of what Roberta thought, he didn't believe for one minute that Hallie was in love with him. In lust—definitely.

But not in love.

Roberta acted as if Hallie had been pining for him all these years. What a laugh that was. Hallie had never been lacking for male attention any more than he'd suffered for lack of female attention.

Roberta's problem was her old-school outlook on life. She hadn't accepted the fact that, yes, it was perfectly normal for healthy men and women to have sex without being madly in love with each other.

Still, she was right about Hallie needing a friend, and not a lover. And she'd need all the help he could give her with Ahn.

Nate was willing to be Hallie's friend, and he was willing to help with Ahn.

He'd do his best to leave it at that.

CHAPTER SEVEN

HALLIE FRANTICALLY CHECKED her watch every few seconds as she paced around the back deck, bouncing a crying baby on her hip. Where the hell was Nate? His cell phone was obviously off since her call had gone straight to voice mail. There hadn't been any point in leaving him a message, however. Nate wouldn't have been able to hear above Ahn's piercing screams.

She'd briefly thought of trying Roberta's cell, before dismissing that option.

If she called after only minutes of being left alone with Ahn for the first time, she'd never be able to live it down.

So where the hell was Nate? Ahn had been crying nonstop practically from the moment Nate and Roberta left. Three hours ago. And Hallie didn't have a clue what was wrong. After they'd waved goodbye to Roberta all of a sudden Ahn's tiny face had screwed up into an angry frown, her lower lip had trembled, then the screaming had commenced.

Hallie had checked her diaper. She'd felt Ahn's head for any signs of a fever. She'd looked the baby over from head to toe. As far as she could tell, there wasn't a single thing wrong.

"Please stop crying," Hallie begged, adding a little more bounce to her jostling.

Ahn only cried louder.

"Oh, look. There's a birdie." Hallie turned Ahn toward the birdfeeder.

Ahn's loud wail sent the bird flapping.

"You want to play in your sandbox?" Hallie cooed, heading for the large plastic pink and green castle that David had set up on the far end of the deck. "You love to play in your sandbox."

Ahn drew her legs up in protest, her feet never touching the sand.

"Poor baby, I know you miss your mommy. I miss her, too. And I promise I'll find you a new mommy. A mommy who will be much better at this than I am. But you have to work with me here, Ahn. I'm doing the best I can. And if you'll just have a little patience, everything is going to get much better than it is right now."

If possible, Ahn's wail reached an even higher octave.

Hallie was on the verge of bursting into tears when Nate's Range Rover finally pulled into the driveway. She hurried down the steps in Nate's direction.

He jumped out of the vehicle, a worried expression on his face as he ran to meet them. "What's wrong?"

"Take her," Hallie demanded, holding the baby out in front of her. "She's been crying since you left."

He looked reluctant, but Hallie pushed Ahn into

Nate's arms anyway. The second Nate took her, Ahn stopped crying, placed her head against Nate's shoulder, and stuck her thumb in her mouth.

"I knew it!" Hallie exclaimed. "I didn't want to believe it, but it's true. Ahn can sense how nervous I am taking care of her. That's why she freaked out when she looked around and realized it was just the two of us."

Nate frowned. "And how did you reach that conclusion?"

"From one of the million baby books I've been reading all week. It plainly states children can pick up on a person's apprehension. It scares them."

"If that were true, she'd still be crying," Nate said. "I'm certainly not comfortable holding her."

"But she obviously feels safe with you."

Ahn snuffled a few times as if to agree.

"You're overreacting, Hallie. Kids cry. They don't need a reason."

Hallie shook her head. "No, I'm right about this. Ahn's having one of those drastic mood swings Dr. Langston mentioned. And I obviously don't have the touch to calm her down."

"Prove it," Nate said, handing Ahn over.

Hallie tensed as she slowly eased Ahn onto her hip. Ahn sniffed again, but didn't break out the tears. She looked at Nate, then at Hallie, her thumb still in her mouth.

"See?" Nate said. "Kids cry. It's what kids do."

"Not this kid," Hallie said. "This is the first time I've

heard her cry. I think she feels safer because you're here and you look like David."

"Or maybe she's just hungry."

"I don't think so," Hallie said. "She ate a pretty good breakfast."

"But now it's time for lunch," Nate said. "Are you hungry?"

"No, Roberta," Hallie said drolly. "I'm not hungry."

"Well, I am. And it's time for Ahn to eat, too. Let's go inside and I'll fix you and I some lunch while you feed Ahn." Nate started for the house, ending the subject.

Hallie quickly caught up. "Okay, Nate. What's going on? You always eat lunch alone at the cottage. So confess. What lecture did Roberta give you on her way home?"

He ignored her question and opened the French doors that led into the house. Hallie entered ahead of him, aware she wasn't going to get an answer. That was Nate's M.O. If he didn't want to answer, he simply ignored the question.

Fine. Let him ignore her. He'd been doing so since the day she met him.

Hallie headed toward the kitchen. The fact that he'd offered to make lunch already confirmed that Roberta had indeed given him one of her lectures on their trip into Boston. And good for her.

After listening to Ahn scream for three long hours, Hallie was desperate for any help Nate offered—today and beyond.

"Would you like some juice?" Hallie asked as she cautiously placed Ahn into her high chair. She promptly took her thumb out of her mouth, which Hallie took to mean yes.

She went to fill Ahn's sippy cup. After the morning they'd had, however, Hallie wasn't looking forward to the lunchtime struggle with the organic peas and carrots on Ahn's recommended lunch menu. She took the baby food jars from the cabinet, placed a scoop of each on either side of Ahn's divided dish, and stirred them with a baby spoon she took from the silverware drawer. Once she'd warmed the vegetables in the microwave, Hallie walked to Ahn, keeping the dish hidden behind her back.

"Juice," Hallie said, placing the sippy cup in front of Ahn. "Can you say juice?"

Ahn picked up the cup and started drinking.

Hallie eased the dish onto the tray and took a seat. Ahn watched her, still swilling the juice.

"That's enough juice for now," Hallie said, taking the cup away from Ahn. "Let's try some peas."

Hallie dipped the spoon into the green goo and angled it toward Ahn's mouth. Ahn turned her head and pushed Hallie's hand away.

Hallie sighed and glanced at Nate, who had a myriad of sandwich items spread out on the island. "I have an idea," Hallie said him. "Why don't you feed Ahn, and I'll make our lunch?"

"Me?"

"Wasn't that our agreement?" Hallie reminded him.

"That we would share the responsibility for Ahn's care?"

"Yes," he said, "but it was your decision that I stay out of Roberta's way all week. You have to give me time to catch up."

"Pay attention, this is real difficult," Hallie said. "Dip the spoon into the food, then put the spoon into the baby's mouth."

"Cute."

Hallie held up the spoon and smiled at him.

Nate didn't smile back. But he wiped his hands on a towel and approached. Hallie immediately abandoned her perch and let him sit.

She didn't immediately take over making their lunch. Instead, she stood behind him, arms folded, smiling to herself. Although he hadn't come right out and said it, she'd gotten the impression he thought she was making too big a deal about the child-care basics. Something about his attitude suggested she was overreacting to the simplest things—such as feeding or changing Ahn. Well, he'd learn. He was about to discover there were few things in life more resistant or spirit-breaking than a stubborn toddler.

Nate picked up the spoon and dipped it into the peas. When he moved the spoon forward Ahn opened her mouth. In the spoon went, and Ahn swallowed.

Hallie gasped. "How did you do that?"

Nate looked over his shoulder. "Pay attention, this is real difficult." He dipped the spoon into the peas and Ahn took another mouthful.

"*Not* funny." Hallie stomped toward the island to finish their sandwiches. Yes, she was being a baby. But she didn't care. It wasn't fair. She'd worked hard all week trying to bond with Ahn. She'd hugged the girl and kissed her and read to her and praised her and changed her and bathed her and dressed her and *tried* to feed her those damn organic veggies.

Hallie watched Nate feed her the freaking carrots.

You little flirt, Hallie thought.

Apparently, Ahn was no different from any other woman. All it took was one look from Nate and she was willing to do anything he wanted.

NATE WAS STILL AMAZED over Ahn's response to him. First, when he held her and she stopped crying, then when she let him feed her.

Maybe her reaction to him really was because he and David looked alike. Deb had mentioned how attached Ahn had become to David. It made Nate regret he hadn't been more involved in Ahn's care until now.

She'd yawned as soon as he finished feeding her, her dark eyes heavy as she tried to fight off sleep. And when Hallie had fretted because nothing had happened on schedule that morning, including Ahn's outside morning playtime, Nate had assured Hallie he would supervise outside playtime after Ahn slept.

Hallie had looked relieved enough to kiss him. Thank God, she hadn't. Instead she'd taken Ahn upstairs for her nap.

Nate lingered in the kitchen, cleaning up, while he

waited for Hallie's return so they could finally eat their own meal. While they ate, he intended to clear up something for his own peace of mind.

"Well, that was easy," Hallie said as she walked into the room. "Ahn was asleep as soon as I laid her down. Probably worn-out from all of the crying."

She placed the baby monitor on the bar and took a seat on the stool across from him. It crossed Nate's mind that Hallie was looking more like her old self every day. She'd gotten a little sun this week being outside with Ahn—she'd always tanned easily and it looked good on her.

Her appearance today reminded him of last summer when he'd been home for a brief stay between assignments. He'd walked up on Hallie and some muscle-bound narcissist sunbathing on the deck. The guy had come with her to visit David and Janet for the weekend. Hallie had been lying on her stomach, the top of her bikini unfastened, the guy rubbing lotion on her sleek, bronze back. His physical reaction, then and now, pushed him to address the issue that had been plaguing him since his discussion with Roberta this morning.

"Are you in love with me, Hallie?"

"You wish," she said and took a bite of her sandwich.

"I'm serious," Nate said.

She looked up at him and swallowed, twice. "Oh. My. God. You are serious."

"ROBERTA THINKS YOU'RE in love with me."

Hallie carefully set her sandwich on her plate. "Oh,

yeah? Well, Roberta also thinks we had a fling ten years ago and that's why I've asked for family leave so I can *play house,* as she calls it, with you. That should tell you how much stock to put in Roberta's theories. But you can relax. I'm not in love with you. I'm only now beginning to *like* you."

"Same here," he said with a grin.

Hallie grabbed her paper napkin and threw it at him.

Nate was quick enough to dodge it.

"Did you really think I was in love with you?"

"No," he said. "And I told Roberta that. But I needed to check with you face-to-face so I wouldn't have any doubts."

"And?"

"You passed with flying colors."

"I suppose I should ask the same. Are you in love with me?"

"No."

"Hmm. I'm sorry, but that didn't sound so convincing to me." Hallie had rattled him and she liked it.

"Hell no, then?"

"Better," Hallie teased. "But with more feeling next time."

His expression changed like flipping a light switch. Nate's voice turned husky when he said, "More feeling is what I'm trying to avoid, Hallie."

Hallie held his gaze. "And how's that going for you?"

He didn't look away. "Hard and slow."

"I bet it would be."

They kept staring at each other. Too long—and they both knew it.

"Okay, you win," he said, pushing back from the bar. "I can't take it."

"You started it," Hallie reminded him.

"And now I'm stopping it."

He took his plate and sandwich with him as he headed for the door.

"I'll call you on the intercom when Ahn wakes up."

He threw his hand up, but didn't look back.

The second the door closed, Hallie picked up another napkin and fanned herself. Nate had made her so hot just looking at her that there was no doubt in her mind the sex would be mind-blowing—something she'd briefly experienced in the back of that taxi.

But passion was fleeting.

Nate was gorgeous. He was brilliant. And he was sexy as hell. But you could stare at a handsome face, listen to an intelligent conversation and screw yourself into oblivion—only so long without eventually wanting something more.

Death had a way of pushing you to examine what you wanted out of life, reminding you of the urgency before it was too late. Hallie had done that this past week. Some things held true. Some things surprised her.

She still didn't see herself married with children or living in the suburbs. Though she realized her career wasn't the be-all and end-all she thought it was—otherwise she wouldn't have put it on hold to take care of Ahn—she knew having a career would always be important to her.

The surprise came when she realized that she could see herself sharing her life with the right man. She'd never admitted that to herself before. For her the right man would love her unconditionally, allow her to be who she was and not try to change her.

Maybe she'd find a guy like that someday. Maybe she wouldn't. Maybe she'd go back to being a producer at the station. Maybe she'd branch out and start a new career.

At this point, there was simply no way to know. There were too many variables and too much that had yet to be decided for her to start planning the next phase of her life.

But she had made one decision as a result of her decision to stay and take care of Ahn. As much as she loved her apartment, it made no sense to keep it. She'd been back to her apartment only once after the funeral to get her clothes, clean out her refrigerator, make sure everything was turned off and unplugged. She would make a trip into Boston soon to make arrangements for her things to move into storage so she could sublet her apartment.

She'd already called her assistant at the station, and Phyllis Ellis had jumped at the chance to assume the lease. The building was located in a choice section of downtown Boston within easy walking distance of the station. And like Hallie, Phyllis didn't own a car.

When you lived in the city, an automobile was more of a liability than it was an asset. Hallie hadn't owned one in years—she hadn't needed to. When she'd wanted to come out to Wedge Pond, she'd either taken the train or caught a ride home with David.

But she did have a car now—Janet's Mercedes. Once Ahn was settled and Hallie signed the house over to Nate, maybe she'd take the Mercedes and keep driving west until she couldn't drive any farther.

Start over?

Or disappear completely?

Maybe, Hallie decided, she would do both.

AS HALLIE HAD PROMISED, she called Nate on the intercom after Ahn woke. He'd been sitting cross-legged on the floor of the deck while Ahn played in her sand castle ever since. She pointed to the bucket closest to Nate. Nate obediently handed it over.

Ahn looked up at him.

And one tiny fraction of Nate's frozen heart melted.

What in the hell am I doing?

This seemingly simple activity threatened the one thing he valued most—his ability not to involve himself with anyone personally.

For the past fifteen years he'd been one selfish son of a bitch, and he didn't regret a minute of it. He'd paid his dues. He'd gotten David out of high school, into college and on his own.

The year after David started college, Nate had reluctantly taken the doctor's advice and stopped trying to care for their mother at home. By then, she'd reached the point where she couldn't be left alone. Although Nate had hired a nurse to stay with her during the day, she'd also needed supervision at night because she'd become so confused she'd often try to leave the house. He couldn't give her that supervision and still hold down a full-time job.

He'd been twenty-five when he'd given up and finally admitted his mother to the nursing facility. And as guilty as he'd felt for doing that, he had found his new liberation exhilarating. For the first time since he was twelve, Nate had enjoyed the pleasure of answering to no one and the freedom to do exactly as he pleased. He'd intended to live that way for the rest of his life.

Until the accident.

The baby pointed to her shovel, snapping Nate from his thoughts. He started to reach for it, but stopped, and regarded her.

"Why you little sneak. I just figured out why you don't talk. You don't need to. All you have to do is point, and adults fall all over themselves to hand you what you want."

Ahn looked at him defiantly. She pointed to the shovel again.

"Say shovel," Nate said. "Say shovel, and I'll hand it to you."

Her answer was to grab the shovel for herself.

"So that's how it's going to be, is it?"

She ignored him completely. Instead, she concentrated on pouring sand carefully into her bright pink bucket.

"Don't worry," Nate said. "I'm not going to tell anyone your secret. A silent woman is a big plus in my book."

"What's a big plus in your book?"

Nate looked over his shoulder to find Hallie walking in their direction. He wisely didn't repeat his words.

"Enjoying the company of beautiful women is a big plus in my book."

Hallie stopped beside him, arms crossed, looking down at the baby. "Well, she's definitely the most beautiful female I've ever seen you with."

"Hey," Nate complained, getting up. "I've dated my share of good-looking women."

Hallie raised an eyebrow. "Like Sherry, Sherry, quite contrary?"

"Well, she *was* a swimsuit model."

"With a brain as tiny as her bikini bottom in that airbrushed photo you proudly passed around the station."

Nate had forgotten all about the woman he'd dated briefly the year Hallie started working at the station. Obviously Hallie hadn't forgotten about Sherry. Just as he hadn't forgotten about the one guy Hallie had dated who had truly gotten under his skin.

"Ah, yes," Nate said. "I'd forgotten you value

intelligence above everything else. Like that Harvard professor you brought to Christmas dinner a few years back. He dominated the conversation and impressed us so much with his brilliance we all fell asleep at the table."

"Touché. I admit Michael was a horrible bore. But we were just friends. We never slept together."

"Shocker," Nate said. "The guy was so in love with himself he didn't have time for anyone else."

"True," she said. "But at least Michael wasn't a psychopath like..." She paused. "What was her name? The one who took a baseball bat to that little red MG convertible you loved because you wouldn't return her calls?"

Nate grimaced. "I'd rather not relive the Gloria situation, if that's okay."

"Shocker." She smiled at him.

Nate swallowed. She'd caught him off guard with that smile. The way she was looking at him with those big brown eyes instantly turned him inside out. That was his cue to leave—now.

"Well, unless you need me to do anything else, I'll head over to the cottage and work on my project."

She smiled knowingly as if she knew exactly how uncomfortable she was making him.

"No, I think we're good for now," she said, but the coy smile wasn't quite gone from her lips when she added, "Dinner will be ready at six as usual."

Nate hesitated. "Look, Hallie—"

"Ease up, Nate. This arrangement isn't going to

work if we can't be ourselves and joke around without you worried I'm going to pounce and ravish you at any minute."

He wished she'd used a different word than *ravish*.

"I didn't think you were going to pounce on me. If you'd let me finish, I was going to say that on weekends when the housekeeper won't be cooking our meals, I don't want you to feel responsible for cooking for me."

"Roberta's already solved that problem," she said. "She left us enough stuff in the freezer to last six months. All I'm contributing tonight is a salad to accompany the casserole I'll be putting in the oven."

"Okay, then. I'll see you at six."

He turned and headed for the steps. Nate could sense she watched him as he walked away. By the time he reached the cottage, he still hadn't recovered from that soul-searching look Hallie had given him.

Who the hell was he kidding? Nate still hadn't recovered from the first time Hallie looked in his direction ten years ago.

CHAPTER EIGHT

HALLIE FOUND IT HARD to believe that it had been four weeks since she and Nate began caring for Ahn on their own, without Roberta. Now it was the middle of June, and even with the help of a housekeeper, Hallie asked herself every day, *What the hell was I thinking?*

As difficult as she'd imagined taking care of a toddler would be, Hallie only wished it were that easy. Had it not been for Nate pitching in, she would have run screaming from Wedge Pond and never looked back.

The most frustrating part for Hallie was Ahn's continued indifference toward her. Although Hallie knew it was silly to even think that way, it was almost as if Ahn were punishing her somehow for not being involved in her life from the very beginning.

Ahn allowed Hallie to dress her, to feed her—provided the meal included pasta—bathe her and even read to her without a fight. She also rarely gave Hallie any trouble when it came to the sleep routine, whether in the afternoon or at night. But when it came to everything else, Nate was the only one who could work with Ahn.

Nate had taken over her stretching exercises, and as a

result, Ahn was walking more instead of expecting to be carried. Nate also made sure she ate her vegetables. He'd supervised all of Ahn's outside playtime—always with a camera around his neck, always taking pictures.

Because of her lingering—and ridiculous—jealousy toward Dr. Langston, Hallie had also abdicated that part of Ahn's care—letting him be the one to take Ahn to her sessions. What did it say about Hallie's personality? That not only would she hate to see the flirtatious banter between Deb and Nate, but also she would equally loathe to see Deb gloat over Hallie taking her advice. And to have Ahn almost completely disregard her in Deb's presence would have been icing on a bitter cake Hallie had zero interest in swallowing.

There were days when Hallie was tempted to return to work and let Nate take over Ahn's care alone, the way he'd suggested in the first place. Yet that was always followed by the desire to prove to Ahn that she was willing to do whatever it took to earn the little girl's trust.

Today was one of Hallie's determined days.

They were finally attending the Monday morning play group. As she sat at Liz Foster's patio table, Hallie didn't know what bothered her most: Ahn ignoring the three other children or the pity Hallie could see in the eyes of the three women sitting around the table. They all engaged in overly polite conversation, but how could anyone overlook the fact Hallie couldn't make Ahn play with the other children? Somehow she suspected all the moms were thinking Janet would know how to get Ahn interacting.

Instead of continuing to pretend there wasn't a proverbial elephant in the room, she decided to address the issue directly.

"I know me being here is awkward for all of you. You don't know what to say to me. So let me make things easier by telling you how I feel about the situation."

All eyes turned toward Hallie.

"I loved my sister. Janet was my best friend. She's always been such a part of my life, it seems ludicrous to me to avoid talking about her."

Liz—the woman Ahn had been with the morning of the accident—was sitting beside Hallie. She was in her late thirties and blonde, and was the first to respond when she leaned over and gave Hallie a hug.

"We loved Janet, too, Hallie. And you're right. It's ridiculous not talking about her." Liz held up her cup of coffee. "To Janet. A true best friend to each and every one of us."

Everyone leaned forward and touched cups.

It should have been comforting, but Liz's comment bothered Hallie. There was no way the relationship Janet had with these women could ever compare with what Hallie had with her sister. Frankly, she didn't appreciate Liz insinuating otherwise.

Still Hallie did begin to relax a little even though hanging out with three women she had nothing in common with wasn't exactly her idea of fun. She was here for Ahn.

"The first time I met Janet was actually online," said a forty-something brunette named Karen. "I'm the loop mom for a chat group for parents who adopt internationally. Janet and I were so excited when we discovered we both lived in Winchester. Neither of our adoptions was final yet, so we became each other's whining post. I brought Austin home from Colombia first. Then Janet brought Ahn home from Vietnam two years later. I have never had a better friend than Janet was to me. She was always there when I needed her, ready to encourage me, or cheer me up, or listen when I had to vent. I miss her every day."

No one had dry eyes after Karen's tribute.

"To Janet," Liz said again and lifted her cup.

Hallie lifted her cup with the others, thinking about those painful years Janet had struggled through Ahn's adoption process. Hallie had tried to be supportive during that time. No. Hallie *knew* she'd been supportive. Yet as petty as she knew it was, she still couldn't help but feel a little pang of jealousy. She knew Janet belonged to this play group, sure, but Janet had never let on she was so close to these women.

"My Janet story is a little different."

Hallie glanced over at Bev, who was seated next to Liz. She looked to be more Hallie's age—pretty, light brown hair, big blue eyes.

"And I hope Hallie can shed some light on the subject. Janet was a serious lingerie freak."

Hallie and everyone else laughed.

"And by *freak* I mean when we would go shopping

Janet would buy all of this fabulous, expensive under-wear that she wouldn't wear because she needed it for what she called her *new* drawer."

"Janet did that even when we were kids," Hallie said. "She always kept one drawer in her dresser for her new stuff. I made fun of her, of course, the way sisters do. But Janet didn't care. She said opening that drawer and seeing all the *new* clothes always gave her a sudden rush of joy."

"To Janet's new drawer," Liz said.

"And to everyone finding something in their lives that gives them a sudden rush of joy," Bev added.

Everyone lifted their cups again.

Hallie decided, of the three of them, Bev was the one she could probably learn to like. At least Bev had included her by acknowledging that Hallie knew Janet better than anyone else.

"My turn," Liz said. "Two years ago I talked Janet into helping me spy on George because I thought he was having an affair."

Karen and Bev died laughing.

"You'd have to know George," Karen said, looking at Hallie. "He worships the ground Liz walks on."

"Whatever," Liz said, rolling her eyes. "Anyway, I got suspicious that morning when George was in the shower and his BlackBerry kept beeping and keeping me awake. I rolled over and grabbed his phone to shut it off and the reminder said meet Carol at two o'clock. Don't think I wasn't sitting up in bed wide-awake when George came into the bedroom to dress."

Bev leaned forward in her chair. "And what did he say when you asked him about it?"

"He said it was to remind him that he had a meeting in accounting that afternoon."

"So why didn't you believe him?" Karen asked.

"Simple," Liz said. "The deer-in-the-headlights look he gave me when I asked him about it. And that's why I asked Janet to drive me, so George wouldn't recognize my car."

Hallie didn't say anything, but she was having a hard time imagining Janet agreeing to spy on someone. The Janet she knew would have talked Liz out of the insanity, not encouraged Liz. But perhaps Hallie didn't know Janet as well as she thought she did.

"We arrived at George's office parking lot by one o'clock," Liz said, "and to my relief his car was still in his parking space. By one-fifteen, I was feeling foolish and Janet was begging to leave. Then, just as I feared, here came George headed for his car. I freaked out. I kept yelling at Janet not to lose him as he drove off. Poor Janet was a nervous wreck as she wove in and out of traffic trying to keep up. We managed to stay two cars back all the way into downtown Boston. And then George suddenly pulled over into a parking space and stopped. I made Janet stop the car right there in the middle of Park Street. The next thing George knew, I was out of the car and in his face."

Liz paused and took a long sip from her cup.

"Well?" Bev demanded. "Don't just leave us hanging."

Liz smiled. "The good news is that Carol was a travel agent at the agency George had parked in front of. Instead of a divorce, I got a lovely trip to Hawaii for our tenth anniversary. We asked Janet and David to go with us and the four of us spent ten wonderful days in paradise. It was truly the best time of my life."

Bev and Karen both dabbed at their eyes again.

In true contrarian fashion Hallie decided maybe a divorce was what Liz deserved for not having more faith in her husband. She remembered the year Janet and David had gone to Hawaii. Hallie had assumed the trip was David's way of getting Janet's mind off the adoption, which was taking so long. Again, Hallie felt slighted that Janet hadn't confided in her about the escapade with Liz. They probably would have had a good laugh about it.

This was her punishment for showing up with a giant chip on her shoulder. She'd been so sure Janet's friends wouldn't like her, she'd ensured they wouldn't with her damn superior attitude. And what had it gotten her? A harsh reminder that, unlike her, Janet did have other friends. Close friends. Friends she had laughed with and cried with and even helped spy on husbands with.

She should have been happy Janet had close friends.

And Hallie would be—eventually—just not right now.

Bev stood, excusing herself for a bathroom break. Karen went to check on her son, who was running around the yard with Liz's little boy and Bev's daughter. And Liz left the table to fill the carafe with more coffee.

Hallie glanced toward Ahn. She'd been checking on Ahn regularly, praying Ahn would at least pay attention to the other children. So far, she hadn't. She was still sitting in the sandbox beneath the jungle gym. Alone. Entertaining herself by pouring sand into a bucket.

Hallie turned to Liz when she came back with a full pitcher. "Does Ahn ever show any interest in the other children?"

"Not yet," Liz said. "But Janet hoped her being around other children would help with her speech and her social skills."

Actually seeing the difference in Ahn and the other children her age disturbed Hallie. Maybe she would take Ahn to her next appointment with Deb Langston, whether she liked the woman or not. Having witnessed Ahn's behavior firsthand, maybe she'd be better able to discuss it with the doctor. There had to be some way to break through to Ahn, and Hallie intended to find it.

Liz sat beside her again. "Roberta mentioned you had already started the search for new parents when I called to invite you to play group a few weeks ago. Any luck yet?"

"No," Hallie said. "But after what Janet and David went through, we knew the waiting game would be the same with the readoption process."

"And how do you feel about the readoption, Hallie?"

"It's what Janet and David wanted," Hallie said simply.

Liz looked concerned. "But aren't you afraid you're going to get too attached to Ahn to give her up?"

It was the second time the subject had come up, first with Roberta's warning, now, with Liz.

"I'm sorry, Liz, but I just don't understand that question. Ahn is my niece. Of course I'm attached to her. But if you mean am I going to get too attached to Ahn to do what's in her best interest, no. I'd never be that selfish."

"When you put it that way, it makes me feel stupid for asking such a question."

"I wasn't trying to make you feel stupid, Liz. I guess I look at this situation from a different perspective. Janet and David wanted Ahn to have *two* parents. I can't give her that. And if the past four weeks have taught me anything, it's what a lousy mother substitute I do make."

Liz reached over and patted Hallie's hand. "I disagree. I've been watching you. You scarcely take your eyes off Ahn. You're a better mother substitute than you think."

Hallie sighed. "You wouldn't have said that if you'd seen me the first time I was left alone with Ahn. She cried nonstop for three hours. I tried everything. Nothing helped."

"Janet had those moments, too."

Hallie was surprised. "Are you serious?"

"She called me in a panic more than once in those early days because Ahn wouldn't stop crying."

"And how did Janet finally calm her down?"

"She didn't," Liz said. "Ahn wouldn't stop crying until David came home."

"Amazing. That's the same thing that happened to me. Ahn didn't stop crying until I handed her over to David's brother."

"I met him at the funeral," Liz said. "He looks like David."

"That was my explanation," Hallie said.

"Is he good with Ahn?"

Hallie hesitated before she answered that question. "Nate's complicated. He's more of a loner than David, who was such a people person. But he has this quiet confidence about him that I think Ahn can sense. She seems to feel safe with him."

"And how does Nate feel about the readoption?"

"The same way I do. Ahn's best interest has to come first. We made that promise to Janet and David when we agreed to become guardians. But I am going to remain Ahn's aunt after the readoption. That's a condition the new parents have to agree with if they want to adopt her."

Liz looked over at her. "And Nate?"

Hallie shook her head. "Nate and I don't agree on that subject. He thinks we should let Ahn bond with her new parents without any interference from us."

"Janet always hoped you and Nate would eventually end up together, you know."

Liz might as well have slapped her.

"Janet never told *me* that," Hallie snapped. "And I find it odd she would say that to you."

"I'm sorry, Hallie. I didn't mean to upset you. I shouldn't have mentioned it."

Hallie was going to be sick. The idea that Janet had discussed her and *Nate* with these women…

She clutched her stomach and stood. "I'm sorry, Liz. I'm really sorry."

Liz jumped up. "Are you okay?"

Hallie waved her away and headed directly for Ahn. Two minutes later, Ahn was strapped in her car seat and Hallie was reversing out of Liz's driveway. A block away from Liz's house, she pulled over to the curb and sobbed against the steering wheel.

She'd talked to Janet every day of her life.

Always.

And that was the problem.

A realization Hallie hadn't fully accepted yet hit her after Liz's comment. And when it hit her, the pain was so sharp, it doubled Hallie over. It had nothing to do with Nate. It had nothing to do with her pangs of jealousy over Janet's close friendships with the other women. It had nothing to do with anything other than the coldhearted truth.

Hallie couldn't call Janet to bitch over what she'd told Liz about Nate. And she couldn't call Janet later to apologize for bitching the way she always did after they had a fight.

Hallie was never going to talk to Janet again.

Accepting it made the unthinkable true.

How long she cried, Hallie wasn't sure. But when she finally pulled herself together, Hallie looked in the rearview mirror. Ahn was leaning forward in her car seat peering out the window as if to scold her for stopping when they should have been on their way home.

"Just give me a second, okay?" Hallie told her.

Ahn leaned back and stuck her thumb in her mouth. And as usual, she refused to look at Hallie at all.

It was another slap in the face.

Only this time, Hallie wasn't going to be ignored.

She unfastened her seat belt and turned around to face Ahn. "What's really the problem with you not talking, Ahn?" Hallie didn't use her calm, patient voice as Dr. Langston's damn notebook instructed. Her tone was firm and it said, *I'm talking to you! Pay attention*—even though Ahn refused to do so.

"You understand every word I say to you. So you tell me? Are you angry about the whole situation like I am? Because if you are, that's okay. You've been jerked around since the day you were born. And if you feel like screaming, you go ahead and scream. Right now, I feel like screaming, too."

To prove it, Hallie let out a scream.

It startled Ahn. She looked at Hallie and blinked. Then she burst out laughing.

Hallie was more than startled. Hallie was thrilled. Ahn had laughed. Her beautiful, nonresponsive, completely detached niece had actually laughed like a normal two-year-old.

"You think that was funny?" Hallie told her. "How about this?"

Hallie screamed a little louder.

This time, Ahn screamed, too.

"You go, girl," Hallie said, clapping her hands in wild approval. "You scream as loud as you want. We've both earned it."

Ahn's next scream was deafening and it was music to Hallie's ears.

She and Ahn had finally connected.

At the moment, nothing else mattered.

WITH HALLIE AND AHN OFF on their Monday morning play date, Nate had the freedom to leave Wedge Pond. In other words, he'd lost his excuse for why he couldn't visit his mother.

While he'd called to check on her daily, the truth was Nate hadn't actually seen his mother in three years. Once she'd stopped recognizing her sons at all, he'd left David in charge of the duty visits.

It was David's turn, he'd told himself. Time David took responsibility for their mother because Nate had been doing it since he was twelve years old.

He'd been sitting in the nursing home parking lot for thirty minutes now, knowing what he had to do, yet postponing the inevitable as long as possible. Nate finally reached for the door handle and walked toward the front entrance of the nursing home.

David had moved her to this facility in Winchester shortly after he and Janet bought the house. It was first-class, always clean, plenty of staff to properly care for the patients.

Nate had called ahead and requested a meeting with the head nurse to go over his mother's daily care. She was waiting for him when Nate approached the nurse's station.

She identified herself as Wanda Thomas. She looked to be in her fifties, was very attractive, dressed in a crisp white uniform, and had every red hair in place. Nate could tell by the way she carried herself Wanda was used to being in charge.

An assumption proven correct when she said, "Let's talk for a few minutes before we go see your mother."

Nate didn't argue with that. He followed her to a vacant sitting area across from the nursing station. They sat in the cozy alcove by the window, surrounded by various potted plants and ficus trees.

"I want you to know how sorry I am for your loss," were the first words out of her mouth. "I had the pleasure of getting to know David and Janet personally. They were fine people."

"Thank you," Nate told her. "I called after the accident to make sure I was listed as my mother's contact person now. And I've checked on her daily. This is the first opportunity I've had to visit."

It was a lie. But it sounded better than the truth.

"How long do you plan to be in town? If I remember correctly, you were out of the country, right?"

"Yes," Nate said. "But now I'll be staying in Winchester indefinitely." He left it at that.

Wanda didn't pry further. "Before you leave today, it's necessary that you stop at our accounting office. There are some papers for you to sign. It's a formality, making you the responsible party for your mother instead of your brother."

"Of course," Nate agreed.

She smiled. "Thank you. Let's go see your mother—we can chat along the way."

Reluctantly, Nate followed as she left the alcove.

"Katharine has really done well on her new medication," Wanda said. "She's less restless, and she doesn't get as agitated as frequently."

Nate frowned. "Is that a nice way of saying she's being heavily sedated?"

Wanda stopped walking and turned to face him. "I don't blame you for being skeptical of how your mother's condition is being managed, Mr. Brock. Alzheimer's disease is one long roller-coaster ride for the patient and the family. Mood swings are constant, up one day, down the next. And yes, there are times when a patient has to be sedated for his or her own safety. But this new medication has been able to keep your mother's temperament at an even keel so far. Hopefully, that will continue."

"I apologize," Nate said. "I didn't mean to imply that she wasn't being taken care of properly."

"No offense taken," Wanda said. "You can ask me any time you have a question. I'll always tell you the truth."

They continued down the corridor until Wanda

paused at a closed door. "This is her room. Don't expect her to recognize you."

"I don't," Nate said. "She hasn't known anyone for a long time."

"But don't let that stop you from talking to her," Wanda said. "She won't remember a thing you've said, but the truth is, Mr. Brock, we encourage our families to talk to the patients mostly for their own benefit. I don't know anyone who doesn't have something they need to say to a loved one, something they've always held back. Tell your mother what you need to tell her. You'll be surprised how much better you'll feel afterward."

As Wanda reached for the door handle, she added, "Just remember to speak in a low, calm voice. And avoid making any sudden movements that might frighten her."

Wanda entered the room ahead of him.

Nate hesitated. When he finally walked into the room, a wave of relief washed over him. His mother was sitting in a wheelchair facing the window. A stark contrast to her position in most of his memories—in bed, her face turned to the wall.

"Katharine," Wanda said, resting a hand on her shoulder, "you have a visitor this afternoon. Your son is here to see you."

Wanda beckoned Nate closer.

Nate walked over and stopped beside his mother's wheelchair. "Hi, Mom. It's been a long time."

She looked up at him briefly. Nate smiled at her and she turned her attention back to the window.

"I'll leave you two alone," Wanda told Nate. "If you need anything, just use the call button."

When Wanda left, Nate pulled up a chair so he could sit beside his mother. She didn't acknowledge his presence again. Nate didn't expect that she would.

"You look good, Mom."

And she did. Funny how the disease attacked only the brain. She'd always been a pretty woman, and she still was. Her face was practically wrinkle-free, her dark hair only sprinkled with a few strands of gray. She was dressed in regular clothes instead of a hospital gown, and Nate was thankful for that, too. She'd spent most of his teenage years in her nightgown, not getting dressed for days at a time.

"I'm glad to see you're sitting up and enjoying this beautiful day."

How many times had he begged her to do that? To get out of bed and enjoy the day? Nate shook his head. Too many times to count.

He reached over and took her hand in his.

Her reaction was lifeless. Just like the look in her eyes.

They sat in silence for a long time, both looking out the window. As the minutes passed an empty feeling that matched the vacant look on his mother's face spread within him.

Then her fingers slowly closed around his.

Everything Nate needed to say came pouring out.

"I'm so sorry, Mom. I was just a kid. I didn't understand that depression was a disease and that you were so sick. And I'm sorry I haven't visited before now. It was easier to let David take over than it was to face that you didn't remember me. So I'm asking you to forgive me. I'm here now. And I'll be here for you as long as you need me."

Those dark days pushed at him now—his anger, his frustration, his fear—and, for once, he let them in. There was one incident in particular that loomed above the others. And no apology he could make would ever take that guilt away.

He'd been fifteen, three years after his father's death. By then he'd taken over complete responsibility for David and his mother. He took care of the banking, depositing the checks from his father's pension and social security they lived on. Nate paid the bills. He did the shopping. He did it all.

Despite his best efforts to hide his mother's depression from their neighbors and his mother's brother, his uncle John began to suspect something was seriously wrong. When John offered to help, Nate was elated. Until Nate realized his uncle's definition of help was to get social services involved.

Nate had pleaded with his mother for days not to let that happen. He'd warned her that she would be committed to a mental hospital, and that he and David would be placed in foster care.

His words had fallen on deaf ears.

The night before the social worker was scheduled to make an assessment visit, he'd made David help him clean the house thoroughly. And after he was sure

David was asleep, he'd gone into his mother's bedroom, grabbed her by the shoulders and shaken her so violently she'd finally sat up in bed.

She'd been terrified. Nate had seen the fear in her eyes. But he'd been too angry to care.

He'd told her if she didn't snap out of it long enough to meet with the social worker, he would never forgive her. He'd promised her if she would do that one thing for David's sake, he'd never ask her for anything again.

Looking back now, Nate had no idea how she managed to pull herself together long enough to meet with the social worker that morning. But she had. And once she'd convinced the woman she was capable of taking care of her family, his uncle John had never interfered again.

He'd never thanked his mother for what she'd done that day. But Nate had thought a million times how differently their lives would have turned out if she hadn't found the courage to fight back, at least for one brief morning, in order to keep their family together.

Still looking straight ahead, Nate said, "Thank you, Mom. You took care of your sons when we needed you most."

He glanced over at her. She'd dozed off, still holding on to his hand.

Nate kissed her fingers before he gently placed her hand on her lap. He stood, bent down to kiss her forehead and then left the room.

Nate had forgiven his mother a long time ago. But he'd never asked for her forgiveness.

Now that he had, maybe he'd learn to forgive himself.

CHAPTER NINE

HALLIE COULDN'T WAIT to tell Nate about Ahn's big breakthrough. But when they arrived home, Nate's Range Rover was missing from the driveway. Hallie looked at her watch. It was twelve-fifteen. He hadn't mentioned he was going anywhere. But then, why would he?

Nate didn't need her permission for anything.

Still, not finding Nate home let some of the air out of Hallie's happy balloon. And that made her think about Roberta's warning again. She definitely had a handle on the situation with Ahn, just as she'd explained to Liz. But was she letting herself become too attached to Nate?

No, Hallie decided as she got out of the Mercedes and retrieved Ahn. *Attached* wasn't the right word— *dependent* was.

She had become dependent on Nate.

And why wouldn't she? Depending on each other was part of their agreement.

With that disturbing thought settled, Hallie headed for the house with Ahn on her hip. The rich aroma of something cooking filled her nostrils the second she opened the door.

Hallie made her way through the den to the kitchen and placed the diaper bag on one of the bar stools. The note she picked up from the counter read:

Pot roast and veggies in the slow cooker on low.
Ready by six. See you tomorrow.
Gladys.

Hallie smiled and set down the note. Gladys Wilson had turned out to be nothing short of amazing. Nate secretly called her "Aunt Bea" because she looked so much like the adorable aunt who ran Andy and Opie's life on *The Andy Griffith Show*—her gray hair always up in an old-fashioned bun, same matronly figure, same penchant for a smooth-running household that included making no bones about how she expected Hallie to keep things tidy in her absence.

Gladys always arrived promptly at eight and left at noon. How she managed to accomplish what she did in four short hours was still a mystery to Hallie. But the house was always spotless, laundry-free and the evening meal taken care of before Gladys left.

"Well," Hallie said, looking at Ahn. "I guess we'd better fix you some lunch, huh?"

As soon as she said it, Hallie glanced at the clock on the microwave. 12:25 and Nate still wasn't home. And lunch meant vegetables. No Nate, no lunch.

Hallie was leaning toward another mac and cheese

meal rather than spoil their big bonding moment, when the door off the den opened. Hallie looked over her shoulder and smiled when Nate walked in.

Yes, she depended on him. And he hadn't let her down.

"Boy, am I glad you're back," Hallie told him. "I was about to cave and let Ahn have mac and cheese for lunch rather than fight her to eat her vegetables."

She'd expected at least a smile out of him, or some kind of quick comeback. When she got neither, Hallie knew something was wrong.

"Are you okay?"

He looked at her for a second. "Why don't we go out for lunch? There's a pizza parlor a few miles away. We could go there and still have Ahn back on time for her nap."

Hallie hesitated. "But we don't know if Ahn will eat pizza."

"There's only one way to find out," he said and headed for the door as if the matter were settled.

Hallie remained still for a second, then picked up the diaper bag again and followed. She had no idea what had put Nate in such a pissy mood—she wasn't even sure she wanted to know. But something told her not to argue with him about going out for pizza. They'd been getting along too well to start a fight over something as trivial as him suggesting that they go out for lunch.

She found him waiting for her when she walked onto the deck. He didn't say a word. He simply took the diaper bag off her shoulder, reached for Ahn, then started down the steps.

O-kay.

Again, Hallie kept her mouth shut. As hard as that was for her to do, she followed along behind him without saying a word. She didn't say anything when she got into Nate's SUV. Not when he put Ahn in the car seat they'd bought for the Rover. And not when Nate backed down the driveway and they headed off to this mysterious pizza parlor that supposedly was only a few miles away. Neither of them said a thing.

For at least two minutes they didn't say a word.

Until Ahn let out a bloodcurdling scream.

"Jesus!" Nate exclaimed and almost ran off the road.

Hallie burst out laughing. Ahn giggled, pleased with herself.

Nate frowned at Hallie. "Care to tell me what's going on?"

Hallie gave him a quick rundown of how all the women sharing stories about Janet had caused her minimeltdown after play group. How she'd screamed in frustration and how Ahn had laughed for the first time. And how they'd both screamed together. How wonderful it had been to see Ahn finally expressing herself instead of giving Hallie her usual disconnected stare.

But Hallie didn't tell him what Janet had told Liz. Or that she'd called Liz on the way home to apologize and to explain why she'd left so abruptly. She was never going to tell Nate that part.

They'd finally reached a point over these past four weeks where there wasn't constant sexual tension between them. On occasion, their eyes would meet and Hallie could feel the heat between them. But for the most part they'd been working extremely well together as a team.

Now that Ahn was showing signs of progress, Hallie didn't want Nate all freaked out over something random Janet had said. Especially not after she'd seen the expression on Nate's face earlier. He'd looked as if he were ready to bolt, like the old Nate who always kept his distance.

"Don't you realize what this means? We're doing something right, Nate. Finally, Ahn's showing some emotion."

"Sounds like we've all had an emotional morning," he said as he pulled into the parking lot.

He got out without expounding any further on that comment. And again, instinct told Hallie to back off. If Nate wanted to tell her what he meant, he would.

She sighed, and opened her door, too. By the time she got out of the Rover, Nate already had Ahn in the crook of his arm, the diaper bag on his shoulder, and was heading for the entrance. He didn't look back to see if she was coming. And he didn't wait for her to catch up.

Hallie stood there for a second with her hands on her hips. *And this,* Hallie thought, *is what married with children would be like.*

She shuddered and followed.

GET 2 BOOKS

We'd like to send you two *Harlequin® Superromance®* novels absolutely fre
Accepting them puts you under no obligation to purchase any more books

HOW TO GET YOUR
2 FREE BOOKS AND 2 FREE GIFTS

1. Return the reply card today, and we'll send you two *Harlequin Superromance* novels, absolutely free! We'll even pay the postage!

2. Accepting free books places you under no obligation to buy anything, ever. Whatever you decide, the free books and gifts are yours to keep, free!

3. We hope that after receiving your free books you'll want to remain a subscriber, but the choice is yours—to continue or cancel, any time at all!

EXTRA BONUS

You'll also get two free mystery gifts! (worth about $10)

FREE!

▲ DETACH AND MAIL CARD TODAY! ▲

NATE WAS USED TO slipping the head waiter a nice tip in order to get a good table in a five-star restaurant, instead of looking around a pizza parlor for a high chair. But even a mom-and-pop joint like this was better than another day of eating lunch as usual.

The same routine was making him restless.

Nate hadn't realized how much he missed his freedom until he was sitting at the nursing home with his mother. Then finding Hallie waiting for him to feed Ahn her lunch had only made him feel more trapped.

Going out for pizza was at least a change.

Nate would take what he could get.

He returned to the table, high chair in tow. As soon as Hallie got Ahn settled, she began looking around, checking things out. Nate hoped she wouldn't show off the new tricks she'd learned. Laughing was one thing. But that unexpected high-pitched scream had scared the living crap out of him.

Funny how this little slice of domesticity also scared the crap out of him.

He was losing his edge. Letting other people suck the life right out of him. Hallie. Ahn. His mother. Everywhere he turned, someone was depending on him. He was beginning to feel the same way he had after his father died.

As if the whole world were sitting on his shoulders.

"What do you think about spinach and cheese for Ahn?" Hallie asked. "That would give her a vegetable."

"You decide," Nate told her.

"Do you want to split a supreme with me?"

"Sure." Who cared what kind of pizza they ate? Or Ahn ate? These weren't life-and-death decisions.

A pimple-faced kid with a phony smile on his face came to take their order. Hallie spoke to the waiter and then looked at Nate. "What do you want to drink?"

"Just pick something," Nate said. "Coke. Water. Whatever." He didn't even pay attention to what she got him.

"I didn't realize until today how far behind Ahn is compared to other children her age. She doesn't even try to interact with other children, Nate. The entire time we were there she never even looked in their direction."

"She's been tested, Hallie," Nate said with more than a hint of groan in his voice. "There's nothing physically wrong with her."

She looked at Ahn again and so did Nate. She was slowly tearing the wrapper off one of the crayons the waiter had given her instead of coloring on the coloring sheet.

It was the same thing she had done at a session with Deb. The doctor's explanation for the behavior was that Ahn had the tendency to focus on small things she could manage. Tiny pieces of paper, for instance, rather than a whole sheet of paper that was overwhelming for her.

Maybe that was his problem, too.

Everything was becoming too overwhelming for him.

"Nate, I hate to even say this—"

"Then don't. Let's just sit here, eat in peace, then we'll go back to the house."

Her angry expression said he'd pushed her too far.

"I have a better idea, Nate. Why don't you sit here and eat your pizza in peace. Ahn and I will go back to the house. And you can find your own way back after you get rid of whatever bug it is that you suddenly have up your ass!"

She held out her hand for his keys at the same time the kid came back to the table with their drinks. It gave Nate the time he needed for a quick attitude adjustment.

"I'm sorry," he said when the kid walked away. "I'm being a real jerk and I know it. I went to see my mother this morning and it left me in a crappy mood."

The anger faded from her eyes. "How is she?"

"The same," Nate said. "But every bad memory I thought I'd forgotten came flooding back the second I stepped into her room. I apologize for taking all that out on you."

She smiled slightly. "I wish I didn't know how hard it is to have bad memories of your parents, but I do. My father didn't have Alzheimer's disease, but he might as well have, for all the attention he paid to Janet and me. I've often wondered if that's why he married my mother's best friend only three months after our mother died. He wanted a strong no-nonsense woman who would dominate our lives so he would never have to deal with us again."

"I didn't realize you had that type of relationship

with your father," Nate admitted. "Or that Roberta had been your mother's best friend."

"Do you think our parents are the reason you and I are so screwed up?"

Nate was surprised by her comment. "You really think we're screwed up?"

"Most people would say so. We don't feel the need to be in a relationship, much less get married. We're committed to our careers. Any friends we have are casual, not long-term. Shall I continue?"

"Are you saying you agree?"

"No," she said. "I think you and I are self-sufficient people who happen to have bad memories about our parents. And I don't think it's fair to blame our parents for anything. Look at David and Janet compared to you and me. We had the same upbringing. And we all had the same choices to make about how we lived our lives. You and I simply made different choices than they did."

"You're basically telling me to put the bad memories behind me and get over it."

"No," she said. "I wasn't talking to you. I was talking to the bug that put you in such a bad mood."

Nate smiled at her. "You think you're pretty clever, don't you?"

Hallie smiled back. "Just one kindred spirit trying to talk another off the ledge, that's all."

They kept staring at each other.

Longer than they needed to be staring at each other.

Fortunately the arrival of the food saved them.

"Okay," she said, changing the subject. "Work your magic. See if you can get Miss Priss to eat her spinach."

Nate reached out and placed a slice of the spinach and cheese on a plate, cut it into small pieces, then waved his hand over the plate until it cooled. Ahn watched his every move the entire time.

"Pizza," Nate told her. "Can you say pizza?"

Ahn looked down at the plate, then back up at him.

"Try it," Nate encouraged. "If you don't like it, we'll get you something else."

Still, Ahn made no move toward the plate.

Nate put a slice on a plate for Hallie and handed it over. "Can you say pizza, Hallie?"

Hallie played along. "Pizza." She took a bite and said, "Mmm. Very good. Thank you, Nate."

"I think I'll have some myself," Nate said.

But he and Hallie were on their second slice before Ahn finally put a piece into her mouth. When she reached for the second piece, Nate looked across the table to find Hallie smiling at him.

"We really are making progress, aren't we?"

"Yes," she said. "We are."

"And us?" Nate said. "We're good now, right?"

"Yes. We're good now."

AHN HAD STARTED SCREAMING at one o'clock in the morning. It was two now, and she was still screaming.

But these weren't breakthrough screams, they were screams of desperation.

Hallie knew exactly how Ahn felt. She finally walked across the nursery and pushed the intercom button on the wall.

"Nate, can you hear me?"

She waited a second and pushed the button again.

"Nate."

"I'm here," he finally said.

"I'm sorry to wake you, but Ahn won't stop crying."

He said he was on his way.

Hallie hurried downstairs to let Nate in. She'd been so sure they were making progress. So sure Ahn was warming up to her. So sure that, finally, she was doing something right.

All Hallie was sure of now was that she couldn't wait for Nate to take over.

Nate walked in and looked at Ahn before his eyes traveled over Hallie's skimpy pajamas.

Every nerve in Hallie's body snapped to attention.

She shook it off. "I'm sorry I had to call you, but she's been crying since one o'clock."

He reached out to take the baby. "Why didn't you call me earlier?"

"It didn't make any sense for both of us to lose sleep."

The second Nate lifted Ahn to his shoulder she put her arms around his neck and held on tight. When her crying slowed to sniffs, Nate looked over the top of

Ahn's head. "Go back to bed." He nodded toward the stairs. "I'll bring Ahn up after she's calmed down."

He was being considerate, and Hallie knew it. But his dismissal made her feel even more irrelevant.

"Go," he said, waving her on.

Hallie didn't have to be told she wasn't needed twice.

She headed for the stairs, pausing on the bottom step only long enough to say, "I have the baby monitor next to the bed, so I'll be able to hear Ahn after you leave. Just remember to lock the door behind you."

He nodded, gently swaying with Ahn to soothe her.

Go back to bed.

How she wished it were that easy. Hallie already knew sleep would be a long time coming. Sleep had eluded her most nights since the accident, leaving her lying alone staring at the ceiling.

She sat on the side of the bed, too tired to be tired if that made any sense. She was tired of all of it. Tired of feeling out of control. Tired of feeling like a failure with Ahn. Tired of feeling dead on the inside.

Janet and David had died in that car wreck. Not her.

Yet she'd slowly been fading into a ghost of the woman she'd been before the accident. She needed to feel *alive* again. She needed assurance that her hopes and wants and needs hadn't been buried along with her sister.

Hallie glanced at the monitor on the bedside table.

Ahn was in her crib, Nate was covering her up. Hallie waited until Ahn's room went dark before she stood and walked away from the bed.

NATE COULD SEE the train wreck coming when he found Hallie standing in the hallway. It was the same train that had been barreling in his direction for ten long years. Only this time, Nate didn't step off the track.

Not when he saw the desperate look in her eyes.

Not when she didn't try to hide her raw, burning need.

"My turn," she said. "I need you to hold *me* now. I need you to hold me and tell me everything's going to be okay."

At that moment, Nate admitted what he'd known all along. He loved her. But he loved Hallie too much not to be honest with her. He walked to where she was standing, her back against the bedroom door leaving only inches between them.

He caressed the side of her face. "If you take me to your bed, Hallie, I can't promise you forever."

"No one can promise forever, Nate. Promise me now."

Nate didn't resist when Hallie took him by the hand and led him into the bedroom. She stopped at the side of the bed, never saying a word as she slowly undressed in front of him.

She stood there, baring herself body and soul.

She was the most beautiful thing Nate had ever seen.

He pulled off his T-shirt and stepped out of his jeans.

And when he got into bed beside her, Nate pulled Hallie close against him, holding her the way she needed to be held, and whispering over and over that everything *was* going to be okay.

He didn't try to rush her. He didn't push her to do anything. He gave her time to decide if she did want more.

She moved closer against him and the feel of her soft, full breasts against his chest made him stir. Her hand slid downward across his stomach, stopping when it reached where he couldn't hide how much he wanted her.

Nate shivered when she touched him.

She rolled on top of him, taking him inside her.

They both moaned when she did.

Nate grabbed her hips, holding her in place as she moved against him, slowly at first, faster as she became lost in her own need. Nate matched her thrust for thrust. He understood her urgency. Felt how desperately Hallie needed to feel the pleasure again in order to forget the pain.

Nate gave her what she needed. Pleasure for the sake of pleasure—nothing else.

But when she cried out, her body quivering as she collapsed against him, Nate rolled her onto her side, cupped her beautiful face in his hands and kissed her tenderly. Now he'd give her what Hallie didn't know she needed. Something Nate needed from her just as badly.

More than meaningless sex.

"I WANT TO MAKE LOVE to you," he murmured.

Hallie moaned when he bent down and ran his tongue slowly around the nipple of her right breast. He took her nipple into his mouth and Hallie pushed his head closer. The sensation was incredible—almost more than she could stand.

"I want to show you how I've dreamed of making love to you from the first time you looked in my direction."

He let his fingers slowly trail down her stomach, past her navel. He parted her legs. And when his finger moved inside her, Hallie fisted the sheets.

"And I want you to know I've never wanted anyone as much as I've always wanted you."

His mouth trailed down from her breast, down to the center of her stomach. Hallie gasped when his mouth moved lower. He parted her legs again, placing them over his shoulders as he lowered his head and placed his mouth against her. Her fingernails sank into his rock-hard flesh as his tongue slid inside her.

He took his time, teasing her, suckling her, driving her crazy as wave after wave of pure ecstasy took her to places Hallie had never been before. And just when she thought she was completely satiated, Nate kissed his way back up her body, making her mad with desire all over again.

"I want inside you now," he whispered. "I want inside you so deep you'll never forget I've been there."

He entered her possessively this time. Claiming what

he wanted. Backing up his threat that she'd never be able to forget him.

Never had Hallie been more turned on.

"Look at me," Nate said.

Hallie did.

"I want you to see how much I want you. I want you to see how much I've always wanted you so there'll never be any doubt in your mind about that again."

He moved slowly at first, taking her with him as he moved faster, increasing the intensity of what they were sharing together. Hallie's eyes never left his face.

It was the most sensual moment of her life, staring into his eyes, finally letting herself feel what she could see Nate was feeling. No holding back. So caught up in each other nothing else mattered except the uncontainable desire that had finally brought them full circle.

He thrust deeper inside her, his own urgency mounting. Faster now. And faster. Bringing them closer to that last final peak. They were so close she could feel it, the pressure of his climax building, her own muscles tightening around him. They were right at the edge now. Right at the edge of no return.

"Now," he said. "Come with me now."

Their bodies came together in one explosive orgasm.

And Hallie stopped lying to herself.

As wrong as he was for her, she was in love with Nate.

Always had been.

Always would be.

HALLIE HAD GONE TO SLEEP only minutes after they finished making love. Holding Hallie while she slept now, her head against his shoulder, his arms around her, had a profound effect on Nate. He'd never allowed himself to experience this level of intimacy with anyone before. He'd always seen intimacy as a threat to his survival. And he'd always seen love as a gamble he wasn't willing to take.

He'd been on the run since he first put his mother in the nursing home and he'd never looked back. He'd done as he pleased and he'd told himself he'd never let anyone tie him down again. What a fool he'd been not to recognize he'd only been running from his own insecurities.

He was forty years old.

And what did he have to show for it?

Very damn little.

The life he'd been living was completely pointless. Putting himself in dangerous situations. Hopping from assignment to assignment. Playing the role of some renegade desperado who didn't need or want anyone in his life.

He thought of how Hallie had looked standing by the bed, unashamed of how much she wanted and needed him.

He thought of Ahn's little arms around his neck, holding on tight, needing him to comfort her because he was the only one who could.

They weren't sucking the life out of him.

They were offering him a chance to love and be loved.

He'd always heard that people eventually reached a crossroads in their life they couldn't avoid. There was no doubt in Nate's mind that he had reached his.

It was time to stop running from love and affection and start giving it. And it was time he stopped worrying about the risk. Loving Hallie would either make him or break him. But there was nothing Nate could do about it now.

The train left the station the second he touched her.

All Nate could do now was hold on for the ride.

CHAPTER TEN

JUNE HAD DRIFTED INTO July and there were times when Hallie would look at Nate and think: *Who are you, and what have you done with Nate Brock?* The transformation in the man who now shared her bed was unbelievable.

Distant and *unaffectionate* no longer applied where Nate was concerned. He proved her point when his arms slid around her waist and he nuzzled her neck as she stood at the kitchen island making a picnic lunch.

"You know you can't do that when Roberta and The Colonel arrive," Hallie reminded him.

"Can I do this?"

He turned her around for a long kiss, pulling her against him so close she could feel how much he wanted her. Hallie put her arms around his neck and kissed him back.

She wasn't going to worry about how long *now* would last. And she wasn't going to worry about what would happen when *now* ended. She was going to enjoy every night she spent in Nate's arms, every kiss he gave her and every moment they spent together.

Hallie finally pulled away from him. "Are you sure a kiss from me is worth Roberta's wrath?"

He grinned. "It's worth it, but I think I'll pass."

"Coward," Hallie teased.

He gave her another quick kiss before he returned to where he and Ahn had building blocks spread out on the floor. Ahn rewarded him with a baby smile when Nate sat down on the floor beside her.

"You're stealing my heart, you little thief," he told Ahn and reached out and tickled her.

Ahn giggled in delight.

Hallie turned her attention back to the picnic basket she was packing. Gladys had prepared them a Fourth of July feast before she left that morning—roasted chicken, potato salad, baked beans…enough for four people instead of only two. So Hallie had invited Roberta and The Colonel to attend the fireworks display with them that evening. It would be the first time Roberta had been to Wedge Pond since Hallie started taking care of Ahn, even though they talked on the phone regularly. Roberta had seemed pleased when Hallie invited them.

Hallie also wasn't going to worry that Roberta had a sixth sense when it came to picking up on things you least wanted her to know. She and Nate had been masters at ignoring each other for years. They could revive that role for one evening.

But as she placed the paper plates and napkins into the basket, Hallie glanced back at Nate and Ahn. One thing that did have her worried was the change in the dynamics between Nate and Ahn now that the three of them were living in the same house.

Nate had always been good with her, and Hallie knew he loved Ahn, just as she did. But the lines were beginning to blur a little, as if Nate had decided to ignore the reality that their time with Ahn was only temporary.

Was it possible Nate would be too selfish to give Ahn up? Hallie didn't have a chance to ponder that possibility further when a knock at the door announced their company had arrived.

Nate was already on his feet, shaking hands with The Colonel. Roberta was bending down to get a good look at Ahn.

"My goodness, Ahn, how you've grown."

Hallie wiped her hands on a dish towel and walked in their direction. "I'm so glad you came," Hallie said, looking first at Roberta, then over at The Colonel. "I thought we'd leave early so we can find a good spot to watch the fireworks. There's plenty of room in Nate's Range Rover so we can all ride together."

"No, it's better if The Colonel and I follow you," Roberta said. "Leaving from Winchester after the fireworks will be closer for us rather than coming back here to Wedge Pond."

Hallie felt like cheering.

And she didn't dare glance at Nate.

Hallie was looking forward to enjoying the evening rather than spending it defending herself for allowing the very thing Roberta had predicted to happen. "Okay, then," Hallie said. "I already have the picnic basket packed and the cooler is on the deck. Give us a few minutes to get things loaded and we'll be on our way."

"I can help with that," The Colonel offered.

Hallie handed the basket over to The Colonel. When he and Nate went outside to load, Hallie looked at Roberta and smiled.

"He's such a nice man, Roberta. I'm glad you have him in your life."

"So am I," Roberta said. "And after you have Ahn settled, I hope you'll get serious about finding someone special, too, Hallie. You deserve that."

Hallie avoided eye contact with Roberta by bending down to pick up the blocks and put them in the wicker basket by the sofa. "Can you say fireworks?" Hallie asked Ahn out of habit.

Ahn's answer was to stick her thumb in her mouth.

"She's still being stubborn about talking, I see."

Hallie stood up and took hold of Ahn's hand. "No, she still isn't talking, but we're making progress every day. My goal is to have Ahn talking by the time we begin interviewing parents."

"I'm proud of you, Hallie. I thought you were making a mistake, but I was wrong. A nanny wouldn't have given Ahn the attention you're devoting to her. You made the right decision."

Hallie was surprised. "Thank you, Roberta."

Roberta had never paid her a direct compliment before.

NATE HAD MOSTLY stayed hidden behind his camera after they arrived at the park. It gave him the distance he needed between him and Roberta.

He snapped a few more pictures as Hallie, Roberta and The Colonel sat on the large quilts they had spread out on the ground. Ahn was sitting in Roberta's lap. Nate snapped another picture as Ahn smiled up at Roberta adoringly. But as he panned back to Hallie, Nate took his finger off the button.

Hallie's feelings were right there on her face. Her dejection over Ahn preferring anyone but her.

Nate lowered his camera. He would give anything if Ahn would grant Hallie that same kind of smile just once. He'd talked to Deb about Ahn's indifference to Hallie, even though he knew Hallie would be furious if she knew that he had. And he'd been surprised when Deb's assessment had been that maybe Hallie was trying too hard to win Ahn's trust, and Ahn could sense that.

But her explanation certainly fit the situation.

There wasn't anyone who could have been more patient, more caring or more loving toward Ahn than Hallie had been over these past months. And for Hallie's sake, Nate prayed Ahn would one day reward her for all her efforts.

He brought the camera up again when Hallie looked in his direction. The look she was giving him was sultry—a promise of what he could expect later. She leaned back, balancing her weight on her hands, knowing exactly what she was doing to him as her full breasts strained against the soft fabric of the top she was wearing.

The little tease.

Snap. Snap. Snap.

Nate would save those pictures for himself.

But Nate almost laughed when Roberta turned to say something to Hallie and she sat up straight. He snapped a few pictures of that, too—her cheeks flushed and guilty-looking.

But at least, Roberta had rewarded Hallie earlier. She'd told Nate on the ride to the park that Roberta had actually said she was proud of Hallie. It made Nate glad he'd encouraged Hallie when she'd mentioned inviting Roberta and The Colonel today.

His mother's illness didn't make it possible for him to turn bad memories into good memories now—other than his satisfaction at being there for his mother instead of running from his responsibility. But Hallie and Roberta still had a chance. And Nate hoped the good memories like the one they were making right now would eventually end some of the tension that existed between them.

"Nate," Roberta suddenly called out. "Put the camera down and come sit with us. It's time for the fireworks."

Nate did as he was told.

He sat down in a cross-legged position on the opposite side of the blanket from Hallie right beside The Colonel. Ahn wasted no time climbing out of Roberta's lap and heading straight for him. Ahn had just settled against him, her head resting back against Nate's chest, when the first of the fireworks exploded across the sky in a burst of brilliant colors.

Oohs and ahhs skipped across the large crowd gathered in the park and everyone applauded in approval. Ahn surprised Nate by putting her little hands together and clapping along with everyone else.

He automatically looked over at Hallie.

She was smiling over Ahn's latest achievement, pushing her own disappointment aside to celebrate Ahn doing one more thing that proved Ahn was slowly making progress.

Nate smiled back at her.

Never had he loved Hallie more.

EVERY NIGHT THAT NATE made love to Hallie was as intense as the first night. But after their lovemaking came their pillow-talk time—time to reflect back over their day or to discuss what they each had planned for tomorrow.

Cuddled in their favorite position—her head on his chest, his arm around her, holding her close—they'd already discussed Ahn's excitement over the fireworks earlier that evening. How Roberta obviously didn't suspect they were living together—it wasn't something she would have kept quiet about. Nate had just finished telling Hallie about the meeting he had scheduled in Boston tomorrow with his associate Dirk Gentry.

Their documentary was already garnering attention even though the film wasn't completed.

"I never expected to get this kind of reaction to the idea," Nate said. "And I don't think Dirk did, either."

"But now that you have received so much attention, you're ready to run with it, right?"

"Absolutely," he said. "I've been thinking about all the doors this film could open up for me. Of course, if someone had told me six months ago I would give up photojournalism for documentary film, I would have laughed in their face."

The huge red flag went up so fast Hallie was almost blinded.

Hallie untangled herself from Nate's embrace and reached over to turn on the bedside light. She brought her knees to her chest as she pulled the sheet up around her.

"That's what you're considering? Giving up photo-journalism altogether?"

Nate sat up to face her, resting his back against the headboard. "Does that concern you?"

"Yes," Hallie said. "If you're thinking about changing careers for all the wrong reasons."

He frowned. "Okay, Hallie. I can already see where you're going with this."

"Good," Hallie said. "We aren't living our own lives right now, Nate. We're living Janet and David's. And it worries me when I think you've forgotten that. Can you really see yourself never going on another international assignment? Because I do not see me continuing this stay-at-home saga and never going back to work."

He ran a hand through his hair. "Truthfully, I don't

know. But I'm not going to lie and say it hasn't crossed my mind that since we're together it might be better to call off the readoption."

"Better for whom, Nate?"

He refused to answer.

"That's the problem," Hallie said. "Ahn deserves better. She deserves parents who have chosen to have children and who don't have any doubts about it."

He sighed. "I know that. But I love that little girl, Hallie."

Hallie leaned over and kissed him. "I love her, too, Nate. I want the best for her, which is why we need to love her enough to be who we're supposed to be to her—her aunt and uncle. We'll always be there for her. Always. But we can't cheat Ahn out of the type of parents she deserves."

Hallie switched off the light.

Nate put both arms around her when she snuggled against him. They stayed that way for a long time. Both awake but neither saying a word.

As she drifted off to sleep, Hallie felt a little better about the situation. She'd told Nate exactly where she stood when it came to the readoption. She'd never let him think because they were together now, she might feel any other way. If she lost Nate in the end, it would break her heart.

But she'd never let Ahn pay the price to keep him.

CHAPTER ELEVEN

IT WAS THE MIDDLE of August—three and a half months since the accident—and Hallie's hope was fading fast. Ahn still wasn't talking. The adoption agency had yet to find any couple willing to take a child Ahn's age with a learning disability. And Hallie's longing for a life free of domestic obligations seemed too stark a contrast to her day-to-day routine to spend much time contemplating it.

Hallie had been in a blue funk all day. But Sunday always put her in a blue funk.

It was a reminder that another long week would begin tomorrow with nothing for her to look forward to but the same mundane routine that was slowly driving her insane.

She walked out onto the deck to call Nate and Ahn in for lunch. Hallie paused for a moment, leaning against the banister as she watched them on the dock.

They were feeding the wild ducks that were abundant on the pond. Nate had squatted down, keeping Ahn safely between his legs while he handed her pieces of bread to throw. The scene should have warmed Hallie's heart.

It didn't.

Out of necessity, they'd become a temporary family. Out of necessity, she and Nate had stopped being who they were and handed their lives over to a two-year-old. And out of necessity, they would keep doing exactly what they were doing until the situation changed.

There were days when Hallie was proud of them for taking responsibility for the niece they both loved. Then there were days like today when she felt as if she were suffocating.

Living in limbo was miserable.

The only thing that kept her going was the *temporary* part. Hallie constantly reminded herself that the way they were living wouldn't last forever. Once Ahn was settled, all three of them would be able to move on with their lives.

What the future held for her and Nate after Ahn, however, Hallie wasn't sure. He hadn't said another word about calling off the readoption. But Hallie couldn't be sure if that was because Nate had realized she was right, or if it was because Nate was holding on to the hope that she would eventually change her mind. Frankly, a part of her didn't want to know because she simply hadn't had the energy to fight about it.

Her current ambitions had been reduced to making it through another day having not pulled out her hair. And finding what solace she could in Nate's arms when night finally rolled around. A far cry from the woman who'd climbed the ladder at the TV station.

There had been some caveats during the past few

weeks. Ahn had finally started to pay attention to the other kids in play group—not outright joining in to play with them, but acknowledging their presence. She was also running as well as walking, and the pediatrician had been amazed at how much progress they were making with her physical therapy. Ahn had even started using a spoon to feed herself. Even better, she was eating her vegetables without having to be coaxed.

That thought reminded Hallie why she'd walked outside in the first place. She called out to Nate, telling them to come in for lunch.

Nate looked over his shoulder and waved, so Hallie walked back inside the house.

She'd already set two places at the kitchen bar for her and Nate. By the time she prepared Ahn's peas and carrots and took Ahn's dish out of the microwave, Nate was coming out of the bathroom off the kitchen with Ahn. He placed Ahn into her high chair and snapped the tray into place.

"Show Hallie your hands," he said. "All clean now."

Ahn, of course, didn't show her hands to Hallie.

She showed them to Nate instead.

But Nate held his clean hands out for Hallie.

And he winked at her when he did.

Hallie rolled her eyes at Nate. But she praised Ahn, placed the food in front of her and handed Ahn her spoon. "Peas and carrots," Hallie said automatically. "Can you say peas and carrots?"

Ahn looked down at the peas and carrots and pushed the dish away. Next, she threw her spoon on the floor.

Hallie raised an eyebrow. "Excuse me?"

Ahn stared her down defiantly.

Hallie slowly bent, picked up the spoon and went to the sink to wash it off. When she returned, she pushed the bowl closer to Ahn and held out the spoon again.

"Be a good girl and eat your lunch. Can you say lunch?"

Ahn slapped her hand away.

Hallie lost it. "Can you say time-out? Because we're getting ready to have a serious chat about time-out, young lady."

Instead, Ahn said, "Pizza."

Hallie dropped the spoon.

When she turned to see if Nate had heard, he was grinning. The next thing Hallie knew, she and Nate were dancing around the kitchen like two idiots. And Ahn was looking at both them as if they were crazy.

They were crazy.

Deliriously crazy.

Ahn had just said her first word.

"This calls for a celebration," Nate said, taking Ahn out of her chair and dancing around the kitchen with her. "If Ahn wants pizza for lunch, I say we go out for pizza."

"Absolutely. You go put her in the car and I'll grab my purse and keys."

As Hallie headed for the stairs, she heard Nate say, "I'd back off on the spoon-throwing if I were you. Aunt

Hallie loves you, but she wasn't kidding about time-out."

Hallie was still smiling over Nate's comment as she grabbed her purse from the bedroom dresser. She stopped mid-stride when the telephone rang. Hallie picked up the phone, and decided to answer when she saw the caller ID.

"Greg, I have great news. Ahn just said her first word."

"I have good news, too," Greg said. "I was out of town Friday and Saturday and I just got around to checking my e-mail. The adoption agency e-mailed me Friday to say they have three couples interested in meeting with you. If it's okay, I'll schedule the appointments for Tuesday, Wednesday and Thursday of this week."

"I can't believe this," Hallie said. "But yes. Of course, schedule the meetings. If the first meeting isn't until Tuesday that will give me time to make arrangements with Roberta to babysit Ahn."

"I'll call you tomorrow to confirm everything," Greg said. "And great news about Ahn, Hallie. I know how hard you've been working with her."

Hallie thanked him, then hung up and tossed the phone onto the bed. But as she headed for the stairs reality set in like a fast-moving thunderstorm.

Nate wouldn't be so receptive to Greg's news. Especially not today.

Not after Ahn had finally said her first word.

Hallie briefly thought of not telling him until after they got back from lunch. Of letting Nate enjoy celebrating Ahn's triumph without the stark reminder that the readoption was finally moving forward.

But she'd never pull it off.

Nate could read her like a book.

Hallie tried to put on a brave face as she walked toward the Mercedes where Nate was waiting. But she'd always sucked at brave faces.

"Greg just called." She held out the keys. "He has three couples for us to interview this week."

Nate took the keys without saying a word.

Hallie was okay with that.

There wasn't anything to say—and they both knew it.

NATE OPENED THE DOOR that still had Holder and Brock, Attorneys at Law painted on the glass at exactly one o'clock on Tuesday afternoon. Greg had told him after the funeral that he was keeping the firm name as a tribute to David.

Nate was making his tribute to David right now—honoring his brother's wishes the way Nate promised.

He ushered Hallie into the office ahead of him, but he felt her stiffen as he placed his hand on her back. He was to blame for that.

They'd hardly spoken to each other for the past two days. Not that Hallie hadn't tried. But Nate flat out wasn't interested in talking the situation to death, and he'd told Hallie so in those exact words.

She hadn't been amused.

Thankfully, Roberta had made the decision for them

when it came to their sleeping arrangements. Instead of waiting until Monday to come to Wedge Pond, Roberta had insisted on The Colonel bringing her Sunday evening.

"Ahn has to get used to me taking care of her again," Roberta had said as her excuse for coming early. "If I spend all day with her on Monday, she should be fine the rest of the week when both of you are gone on the interviews."

Nate said hello to the receptionist, who told them Greg wanted to see them in his office before the interview. She pushed the intercom button on her phone and announced their arrival. Then she showed them to Greg's office door.

Greg was on his feet the second they walked in. He and Nate shook hands and Greg motioned for them to take a seat in the chairs facing his desk.

"Don't be nervous about this interview," Greg said. "There's no pressure here. The purpose of this initial meeting is strictly so you can be introduced to the couple in person."

"And then what?" Nate asked.

"If you like them, you request a second interview," Greg said. "And the second interview is usually where you'll introduce the couple to Ahn."

Nate frowned. "That seems a little soon to me."

"You can use your own judgment about that, Nate," Greg said. "But remember, adoption is a two-way process. The adoptive parents are going to want to see the child as much as you want to get a good look at the adoptive parents."

Greg looked at Hallie. "I didn't get the information on the three couples you'll be interviewing until this morning. I'll have my secretary scan and e-mail you the dossiers on your Wednesday and Thursday appointments so you'll have time to look them over. But I'll give you a quick rundown on the Wobacks before you meet them."

Greg picked up a sheet of paper. "Bill and Shirley Woback are both thirty-eight and they've been married ten years. Shirley is a registered nurse, but she plans to stay home once they adopt. Bill is an insurance executive who has banker's hours, so he's ready to become a hands-on father. They're actively involved in the Methodist church they attend. Bill is a member of the Rotary Club. Shirley volunteers at a free clinic twice a month. Their parents are still alive, so Ahn would have two sets of grandparents. Bill has two married brothers, both with children. Shirley has one married sister, but no children yet. There are no divorces on either side of their families."

Hallie spoke up for the first time since they'd entered the office. "They almost sound too perfect, don't they?"

"That's the point of the personal interview," Greg said. "People can seem great on paper. It's meeting them in person that counts."

"And they understand our situation?" Nate quizzed.

"Yes," Greg said. "This is an open adoption. Everything has been fully disclosed to the three couples you'll be interviewing this week, including Hallie's desire to maintain her relationship as Ahn's aunt."

"And what if I decide to remain Ahn's uncle?"

"I can't see how that would be a problem," Greg said. "None of these couples had any objection to Ahn's family staying in touch."

"Good," Nate said.

"Are there any other questions before I take you to the boardroom to meet the Wobacks?"

"Yes," Hallie said. "I read over the agency's guidelines for the interview process. I made a list of questions, but truthfully, running down a long list seems so impersonal to me. Do you have any other suggestions for how we should do this?"

"My best advice is to do what feels comfortable to you. Maybe switch it up. Take turns asking questions. Eventually you'll start having a conversation instead of conducting an interview."

"Good advice," she said.

Greg stood. "Then if you'll excuse me, I want to introduce myself to the Wobacks before the interview. I'll be back to get you in a minute."

Hallie pounced the minute Greg left the office—just as Nate figured she would.

"What do you mean *if* you decide to remain Ahn's uncle, Nate? Just because you're mad at me, don't take it out on Ahn. Of course you're going to stay involved in Ahn's life. Whatever happens between us has nothing to do with you staying in touch with our niece."

Nate looked over at her. "And what to you mean by *whatever happens between us,* Hallie? After you get Ahn out of your hair, am I going to be next?"

He seriously thought Hallie was going to slap him.

Greg saved Nate from finding out.

"Ready?" he asked when he opened the door.

Hallie marched out of the office without looking back. Nate sighed and followed. Of course they were on edge with each other. They were holding Ahn's future in their hands. And their first interview made all of it real.

He thought about Ahn's progress.

She'd said her first word on Sunday. And she'd said her first sentence this morning after breakfast while they were feeding the ducks. She'd said, "Stop ducks," when two of the larger ducks kept pushing a small duck away.

It was the same thing he and Hallie were doing now.

Two large ducks pushing the small one away.

Nate wanted to grab Hallie by the arm and march her right back to Wedge Pond. He wanted to make her see that they could raise Ahn the same way they had been doing—quite magnificently, if he had to say so himself.

But Nate already knew he couldn't *make* Hallie do anything. His only hope was going through with the damn interviews so Hallie would see for herself that the only parents Ahn needed were the ones she already had.

His hope began fading fast, however, when Hallie breezed into the boardroom with a big smile on her face as if she were greeting long-lost friends. Friendly was the last thing Nate was feeling.

But he had to admit the Wobacks were a nice enough looking couple. At least, the wife looked normal—pretty, blonde, nicely dressed.

The husband was a different story. The guy had shifty eyes, as if he had a secret you might discover if he looked at you too long. Nate could already see the sweat beads popping out on his brow below his receding hairline.

Yeah, this guy had something to hide.

Serial killer? Sex offender? Baby broker? Who knew?

Greg made the introductions.

Nate nodded curtly to Shirley.

But Bill's handshake was limp and as damp as a dishrag. Nate had to suppress the urge to wipe his hand on the side of his pants.

When they all were seated, Hallie wasted no time getting to the point. "I think this will be less awkward if we take turns asking each other questions."

"I agree," Nate said. "Tell me why you're ready to be a father, Bill."

Hallie kicked him under the table.

Bill took a handkerchief from his inside coat pocket

and blotted his forehead. He still wouldn't look directly at Nate for more than a second at a time.

"Well," he finally said, "I'm very close to my family. And family has always been important to me. I guess I've always been ready to be a father. I just haven't been given that opportunity yet."

Nate pressed further. "And the family you're so close to is on board for the adoption?"

He sat up a little straighter. "Yes. Shirley and I both made sure our families would be receptive to an Asian child before we requested the interview."

Nate didn't say anything after that.

He didn't even listen to the questions Hallie was asking them. Nor did he really pay attention to the questions they were asking Hallie.

Nate was forced to shake hands with Bill again after the interview was over. As soon as the Wobacks left the boardroom, Nate did what he'd wanted to do the first time he saw them. He wiped the Wobacks off his list the same way he wiped his hand off on the side of his pants.

"I DON'T THINK I've ever been more embarrassed," Hallie fumed as she stomped to the Ranger Rover ahead of Nate.

She slammed the door after she got into the car. When Nate slid behind the wheel, he slammed his door, too. Yeah, they were acting childishly, but she was too angry to care at the moment.

"I cannot believe you were so rude to those people. There's no excuse for it."

"I didn't like the guy, okay? He had shifty eyes."

"He did *not* have shifty eyes. You have a way of intimidating people, Nate. You're so damn confident you suck all the air out of a room the second you walk into it."

Nate's head jerked in her direction. "You're really taking up for the guy after his comment about talking with their families to make sure no one had a problem with them adopting an Asian child? Unbelievable."

"He was trying to assure us no one had a problem with Ahn's race."

"That's bullshit," he argued. "If they didn't have a problem with Ahn's race, why would they feel the need to talk it over with their families? Did David and Janet call you to discuss their decision to adopt a child from Vietnam?"

Hallie sighed. "You know they didn't."

"Exactly my point."

"Okay," Hallie said. "You're right about that. But if this is the way you're going to treat the people we interview, we'll never find parents for Ahn. And if that's your goal, Nate, you really disappoint me. Never in a million years would I have thought you would be so selfish."

"Fine," he said. "I'll let you do all the talking at the next interview tomorrow."

"Thank you," Hallie said. "I will."

Nate went straight to the cottage the second they

arrived at the house. Hallie didn't try to stop him. She was even thankful that Roberta being there forced them to be apart while they were going through the interviews.

If she and Nate needed anything, it was time alone right now. Since the accident, they'd been together non-stop. And their routine had been anything but normal. People didn't live the way they'd been living—not even Janet and David. Two adults staying home all day, their only focus on the child they were taking care of together simply wasn't normal.

Nate had at least had an outlet with his damn documentary. But even that didn't count. Not really. The only time Nate took a break to look through his photos was while Ahn was taking her nap.

Did he really call that living?

Well, sorry, but she didn't.

Hallie had herself so worked up by the time she walked into the house, she couldn't hide it. She found Roberta and Ahn sitting on the sofa, a book between them.

Roberta took one look at her and said, "Well, I don't guess there's any point in asking how the interview went."

Hallie kicked off her heels and flopped into the recliner. "Then ask me how the interview would have gone if Nate hadn't made a complete ass of himself."

"You had to know this wouldn't be easy, Hallie."

"I know," Hallie said. "But Nate never gave the

couple a chance. If he isn't in a better mood tomorrow, I'm not taking him with me to the interview."

"Sounds like someone else needs to get in a better mood," Roberta said. "Go have some quiet time and calm down before dinner. You're interrupting our story and we're just getting to the good part."

Hallie picked herself up from the recliner, grabbed her shoes and stomped toward the stairs. Thank God Roberta was here for the next three days. At the rate they were going, she and Nate would kill each other before the interviews were over.

Turning Ahn over to Roberta was the equivalent of a guilt-free pass. It made Hallie wonder if she'd ever be able to feel the same way about the readoptive parents if they did choose a couple. Logic told her she would. Hallie's heart feared she wouldn't. And experience told her only time would tell.

But Hallie wasn't going to worry about any of that right now. She was going to take a nice, hot bath and try to pull herself back together.

She couldn't expect Nate to be logical if her emotions were all over the place. And she couldn't expect him to be civil if she were being nasty to him.

She loved him.

And she loved Ahn.

With all her heart, Hallie loved them both. She needed to figure out how to prove to Nate that doing what was best for Ahn also meant doing what was best for them. Ahn needed a new start in life, just as she and Nate needed their lives back. Only then would they all be able to put the past behind them and move forward together.

Forward for Hallie meant forward *with* Nate and Ahn.

Not *without* either of them.

Why couldn't Nate understand that?

Hallie sighed as she undressed. As the tub filled she realized how exhausted she was. It was the first time in what seemed like forever that she really could take a bath and go to bed early if she wanted without worrying about anyone or anything other than herself.

God, how Hallie would love to do that.

And she didn't care that it was only five o'clock. She needed some space. Some me time. Some get-her-head-on-straight time. She'd earned it. And she was going to take advantage of having the opportunity to be rewarded for what she'd earned.

NATE PACED THE COTTAGE like a caged animal, stewing over everything that had happened that afternoon. Hallie had called him selfish, intimidating and rude. And everything she said described exactly how he'd acted today during the interview.

Nate was ashamed of that.

But he wasn't going to retract his initial impression of Bill Woback. Nor had he been wrong that the man's comment about Ahn's race had been completely unacceptable and totally offensive.

But Nate would to do things differently tomorrow.

He was going to leave tomorrow's interview completely up to Hallie. He would sit there politely and never say a word—that was what Hallie wanted anyway. She wanted him to do exactly what she told him to do and like it whether he did or not.

But wasn't that what he'd been doing so far? Still Hallie wasn't satisfied.

She'd said she was disappointed in him. Well, his disappointment in her was double. If she really wanted to discuss the selfish issue, Hallie needed to start with a good look at herself.

Nate walked to the kitchen, grabbed a beer and stomped back across the great room. When he flopped down on the sofa, Nate drained half of the bottle in one angry gulp.

What a fool he'd been.

He'd let his guard down and ignored the one thing he'd always known to be true. Life never let you keep the things you wanted most.

What Nate wanted most was Hallie *and* Ahn. And he had a good chance of losing them both.

Nate took another long swig from the bottle, already deciding he was not going to the main house for dinner in an hour. Nate got up from the sofa and walked to the intercom.

He hoped Hallie would answer. Hoped she would hear in his voice just how disgusted he was with her, too.

Nate got Roberta instead.

"I'm really not hungry tonight," Nate told her. "So don't worry about dinner for me."

"I guess that means Ahn and I will be eating alone tonight," Roberta said. "Hallie just came downstairs and told me the same thing."

Nate grimaced at the loud click.

So Hallie had no interest in seeing him tonight, either. Fine. He needed a break from her, too.

Nate walked to the refrigerator for another beer. But as he slumped on the sofa again, he could already hear the haunting whistle of a fast-moving train.

Maybe he should lie down on the track this time and finally get the train wreck over with.

CHAPTER TWELVE

HALLIE WAS GLAD the second interview was scheduled for ten o'clock on Wednesday morning. She desperately needed to talk to Nate—privately—so she couldn't wait to leave Wedge Pond that morning. Hopefully she could straighten things out between them.

Her blissful night of having no one to worry about hadn't gone so well. She'd awakened more than once during the night to check the monitor that wasn't there because Roberta had it with her in the guest room. When she'd reached for Nate and he wasn't there, the miserable feeling in the pit of her stomach made her sick. That was when Hallie realized she couldn't make it through another day with them being so angry with each other.

Nate was in the kitchen having coffee with Roberta when Hallie came downstairs. Ahn was eating her cereal and Hallie could hear Gladys in the laundry room already starting up the washing machine.

"Good morning, everyone," Hallie said cheerfully and walked over to kiss the top of Ahn's head.

Ahn didn't acknowledge her at all.

Nate barely mumbled, "Good morning."

And Roberta said, "You'd better get going if you're going to be on time."

Hallie couldn't have agreed more with that suggestion.

Nate slid off the stool, then kissed Ahn. She looked up and smiled at him. Hallie was surprised when Nate looked over at her next.

"Ready?"

Nate even waited for her to collect her purse before they headed for the door together. His actions gave Hallie hope he was tired of fighting, too.

"We'll be back as soon as possible," Hallie called over her shoulder to Roberta.

"Good luck with the interview."

They hadn't even made it to the Range Rover when Nate said, "I want to apologize for yesterday."

"So do I."

They climbed in and Nate put the car in gear, then backed down the driveway.

"I don't blame you for being confused, Hallie. We were both in agreement with the readoption in the beginning. And I know your opinion hasn't changed. But right now I'm having serious doubts."

"What can I do to help you put those doubts aside?"

"A little understanding, maybe?"

"Understanding goes both ways, Nate. You act as if I'm tossing Ahn aside, and you know that isn't true. I told you from the beginning that I want to be a part of

Ahn's life. I'll always feel the need to be able to check on her."

"And I guess that's where I'm having my doubts," he said. "I'm not sure I could ever trust anyone else to take care of Ahn. Even if I do have the right to check on her."

"But what if we could find a couple who you knew beyond a shadow of a doubt that you could trust? Would you still feel the same way?"

He glanced over at her again. "That would be a completely different story, Hallie, and you know it."

"Then all I'm asking is for you to walk into these interviews with an open mind, Nate. Maybe you're right. Maybe we'll never find a couple we trust. But maybe I'm right, and we will. At any rate, we both owe it to Ahn to try. That's all I'm asking."

"Okay. I'll walk into this interview with an open mind."

"Thank you." She waited for a few seconds before asking, "And us? Are we good now?"

"We've been better."

Not much of an answer but Hallie would take it for now.

She reached into her purse and pulled out the e-mail Greg's assistant had sent her on couple number two—Harvey and Gwendolyn Brown. "I only glanced at the information Greg sent us on this morning's couple, and I know you haven't had a chance to look at it. Would you like me to give you a rundown the way Greg did for us yesterday?"

"My mind is wide-open," he said with very little enthusiasm.

Hallie ignored his cynicism. "The Browns own a property rental company, as well as owning all of the rental properties they manage. She's older, thirty-eight. He's thirty-two. They've been married seven years, and this is the first marriage for both of them."

Hallie paused, reading over the information. "It appears Gwendolyn is the more active of the two when it comes to community involvement. There's a long list of organizations she belongs to, and she's the chairperson on several different committees."

"So when would she find time for Ahn?"

"That's a question we can ask her."

"That's a question *you* can ask her," Nate said. "I told you yesterday I would let you handle this interview."

"What happened to your mind being wide-open?"

His expression was serious when he looked over at Hallie. "I'll keep an open mind. You've already convinced me I need to do that."

NATE'S MIND MIGHT HAVE been wide-open, but Hallie's mind snapped shut almost from the second they walked into the boardroom. The Browns were the most mismatched-looking couple Hallie could imagine.

The first word that crossed Hallie's mind for Gwendolyn was *Amazonian*. She had a commanding presence, her dark hair pulled back in dreadlocks, and her hard, chiseled features were representative of a warrior who might consider eating her children if it was necessary for her own survival. Husband Harvey barely came to Gwendolyn's shoulder. And Hallie couldn't help but notice the man bore a striking resemblance to Pee-wee Herman.

Hallie didn't have an opportunity to say a word after Greg made the introductions. The minute Gwendolyn sat she pulled out a list. She ignored both men and focused solely on Hallie.

"Does the child sleep through the night?"

"For the most part, yes," Hallie said. "*Ahn* sleeps through the night."

"Is she potty trained?"

"No," Hallie said. "But we're working on that."

Gwendolyn immediately looked over at Harvey, who obediently scribbled something on the notepad in front of him.

"Does the child have any food allergies?"

"No," Hallie said. And again she stressed, "*Ahn* doesn't have any food allergies."

"Is she allergic to pets?" Gwendolyn asked. "Because it's only fair to tell you that we have three dogs and four cats that *will* stay part of our family. That isn't negotiable on our part."

"And it's only fair to tell you that I have no idea if Ahn is allergic to pets. We have no dogs or cats."

Gwendolyn looked over at Harvey. He made his notation on the pad again.

"Are the child's immunizations up to date?"

Hallie was over it. "Her name is Ahn. And yes, all of

Ahn's immunizations are up to date." Hallie's curtness didn't even faze Gwendolyn.

"The adoption agency noted delayed developmental issues. Is that a nice way of saying she's mentally retarded?"

Hallie's head jerked toward Nate sitting beside her. *Now* was the time for him to be rude and obnoxious.

Nate just looked at her, an amused smile on his lips.

Hallie faced Gwendolyn. "You know, now that I think about it, the reason my sister and brother-in-law didn't have pets is because Ahn does have a severe allergy to pet dander. Sorry, but the dogs and cats will have to go. And that isn't negotiable on our part."

Gwendolyn stood and Harvey snapped to attention with her.

"This interview is over," Gwendolyn announced.

She glared at Hallie and gave Pee-wee Harvey a hard push toward the door.

Hallie waited until the Browns had cleared the threshold before she turned to Nate. "Don't you say a word. I mean it. I'm too upset right now."

Wisely, he didn't.

He waited until they reached the SUV. "Maybe we should keep an open mind about what happened and schedule a second interview so we can introduce Ahn to the Browns."

"*Not* funny."

"None of this is funny, Hallie. None of it. Especially not what this is doing to us."

They were in each other's arms so fast neither of them cared that they were standing in the middle of a public parking deck. The next thing Hallie knew, Nate had her pushed up against the car and her hands were tangled in Nate's hair as his mouth came down on hers in an urgently violent kiss. His hands gripped her hips, pulling her against him so she could feel how much he wanted her.

"Get a room already," someone yelled out from several cars away.

They instantly pushed away from each other.

Nate grinned. "Why didn't I think of that?"

IT WAS WELL PAST two in the afternoon before Hallie walked up the steps to the deck. Roberta sat at the patio table, thumbing through a magazine, the baby monitor in front of her on the table indicating Ahn was still down for her nap. Roberta purposely looked at her watch, then back at Hallie.

"That must have been some interview."

Hallie blushed. "Don't start with me."

"I just have four words to say on the subject," Roberta said when Hallie took a seat beside her. "I told you so. And don't think for one minute I've been fooled about what's going on. I'm the one who arranged for the charity to pick up Janet's and David's clothes the day you went to close up your apartment. So don't try to tell me those are David's clothes hanging in your closet. I saw your housekeeper put away Nate's clothes in your room without question on Monday after she finished the laundry."

Hallie rolled her eyes.

"But speaking of words," Roberta said, changing the subject now that she'd thoroughly chastised Hallie, "I said the wrong word earlier when I was reading to Ahn. I called the pig in the story a piglet. And Ahn looked up at me and said, 'Say pig.'"

Hallie laughed.

"There's nothing wrong with that child's mind, Hallie. She has a stubborn streak, just like you."

"Me?" Hallie echoed.

"Shall I count the ways?"

"No. I'm sure you'd manage to work Nate in there somewhere, and that's a situation Nate and I still have to figure out for ourselves."

"And the interview?"

Hallie groaned just thinking about it. "It was a disaster. The wife was the most obnoxious woman I've ever met, and the husband was so browbeaten I actually felt sorry for him."

"I thought the adoption agency was screening these people for you."

Hallie sighed. "Their qualifications looked great on paper. But that's why a personal interview is necessary."

"Don't look so disheartened. You still have tomorrow's interview. It's at ten o'clock in the morning, too, isn't it?"

Hallie nodded.

"But if you're going to be late tomorrow—"

"I promise," Hallie cut in. "We'll be back on time."

"See that you do," Roberta said. "The Colonel and I have dinner plans tomorrow night. He's taking me to a new restaurant and we've waited weeks to get a reservation."

Roberta didn't have to worry about them being late.

Hallie had her own plans for tomorrow night.

All night—with Nate back in her bed.

AFTER NATE DROPPED Hallie at the house, he left for his weekly visit with his mother. It had ceased to matter that she had no idea who he was, or that she seldom acknowledged he was there. Nate knew he was there. And today he had a lot on his mind.

Wanda had been right when she'd told him the visits were as much for the family members as the patients. Being able to tell his mother anything was better than any therapy session money could buy.

She was, after all, his mother.

He should be able to tell her anything.

When Nate reached her room, he was relieved to see she was sitting up again today. He'd bought a bird feeder and placed it outside her window. She seemed to be watching the bright yellow finches sitting on the perches pecking at the seeds. At least, Nate liked to think she was enjoying watching the birds at her window.

"Hi, Mom," he said, kissing the top of her head.

She looked at him briefly, then back at the feeder.

Nate positioned a chair next to her wheelchair and took hold of her hand. The routine had become so comfortable for him he saw no reason to change it.

He started the usual one-sided dialogue he exchanged with his mother, but he suddenly paused. Was that why he was having doubts about going through with the re-adoption? Had his daily routine become so comfortable for him that he saw no reason to change it?

"I'm confused, Mom. All those years I took care of you and David I told myself that when David grew up and when you got better, I'd never take care of anyone else again.

"I felt so cheated, Mom. I didn't have the freedom other kids my age had. Sports were out of the question even though I was a damn good first baseman. And forget dating. You don't ask a girl for a date and expect her to hang out at your house while you cook dinner and help your little brother with his homework. Did you know I was a virgin until I was twenty?

"It was the summer I won the Kodak amateur spot news photojournalism award. David was away at church camp. And Uncle John agreed to stay with you for the weekend while I went to New York for the award ceremony.

"I got a little drunk for the first time at the awards' banquet. And it gave me the courage to hit on this brunette sitting at the same table. She was older than I was, maybe twenty-four or twenty-five. She definitely took pity on me in more ways than one.

"But, you know, taking care of David's daughter

has been a different experience for me. I've enjoyed it, spending time with her. I don't know if it's because I'm older. Or if having my freedom for so long has made it less important to me. Maybe I've enjoyed it so much because of how much I love Hallie.

"I know you don't remember Hallie, Mom. But you've met her. She came with David and Janet. She's mentioned coming with me, but I'm not ready for that yet. I think you and I need a little more alone time before I start bringing visitors.

"But you would like her. She's smart and funny, and she's so beautiful it's hard for me to breathe sometimes when I look at her. But I guess what I like best about her is that she tells me exactly what she thinks. Like with the readoption. Hallie doesn't have any doubts it's in Ahn's best interest to find her new parents.

"The funny thing is that I felt exactly the same way at first. It was crystal clear in my mind that the only right choice was to do what David and Janet asked us to do. For Ahn's sake, I believed it was our duty to put her up for readoption.

"But now, the thought of anyone other than Hallie and me raising her is like a knife right through my heart. I keep wondering what will Ahn think if I'm not there to comfort her when she's crying. Or will she wonder what happened to pizza night on Fridays and feeding the ducks every day? And after her bath when it's time for stories, will her new father take time to let her climb into his lap and hold on to his two fingers while he reads the same book not once, but twice?

"This child has been through so much already. You can see it in her eyes when she looks at you. You can see her trying to decide if she should trust you or if you're like everyone else who has disappeared on her. That's why the thought of her being taken from the only real home she's ever known and handed over to strangers seems unfathomable to me.

"Hallie says we need to love her enough to find her good parents, so we can be who we're supposed to be to her. Her aunt and her uncle. But I'm not sure I can do that, Mom. If we go through with the readoption, it may have to be a clean break for me. Worse than me not having any contact with Ahn, would be the chance that every time I looked into her eyes there would always be that big question staring back at me. 'Why did you give me away?'

"So, what do you think, Mom? Should I be selfish and keep Ahn regardless of what Hallie wants and regardless of what's really best for Ahn? Or should I do what David asked me to do and find the best parents for his daughter?"

Nate wasn't expecting an answer. It was talking things out that helped.

CHAPTER THIRTEEN

HALLIE AND NATE had both vetoed the third couple they'd interviewed several weeks ago. The wife had been so shy she barely said hello. The stockbroker husband had excused himself every few minutes to take an important call from one of his clients. His actions told them exactly how important Ahn would be to him if he couldn't even stay off the phone long enough for the interview.

Now August had turned into September with no prospects on the parental front. It made Hallie worried.

Worse, she'd had nothing but bad news all week. First, from Greg, letting them know that the adoption agency had exhausted their nationally linked applicant file and had no other couples who met their qualifications.

Second, Nate had dropped a bomb on Hallie after Ahn's latest session with Deb. According to Deb, unless they were able to find adoptive parents for Ahn by her third birthday, she would strongly advise against the readoption. Apparently by age three, Ahn would reach a critical stage where another major life change could be so traumatic for her that she might suffer serious emotional issues for the rest of her life.

Ahn would turn three in February.

That left four short months to find new parents, and Hallie wasn't stupid. The chance of that happening would be nothing short of a miracle.

Hallie glanced at Ahn, playing in the yard with Liz's son. Liz had stopped by to return some of Janet's silver serving pieces she'd borrowed for a dinner party and had stayed for a visit. They sat on the deck, sipping iced tea, while Ahn ordered Jacob around, giving him strict instructions about what he could and could not do with her toys.

Ahn had gone from not talking to talking nonstop. And boy, had she turned into a bossy little thing. Nate, of course, was wrapped around Ahn's little finger. That meant Hallie had to be the disciplinarian—so *not* her favorite new role.

Time-out was employed at least once a day because Ahn was so stubborn and often refused to do what she was told. The second she'd served her sentence, she ran straight to Nate, her lip pooched out at Hallie for putting her there.

Hallie had vented to Roberta about the situation more than once. And Roberta always reminded her that the hardest part about being in a mother's role was having to be the bad guy.

Given the current circumstances, it appeared Hallie was going to become Ahn's mother whether that had been her intention or not. She and Nate had talked extensively after the session with Deb on Tuesday. Hallie had agreed that rather risk the chance of any permanent emotional damage to Ahn, who had already suffered so much, they would call off the readoption if they hadn't found parents by her third birthday.

"Am I wrong, Hallie? Or are you a million miles away today?"

"Sorry, Liz. I guess I am."

Liz looked at her thoughtfully. "Thinking about Janet?"

"Would you think I'm terrible if I told you I was thinking that I'd really like to be me again, instead of Janet?"

"I don't think you're terrible at all," Liz said. "It has to be overwhelming stepping into your sister's life like this. Taking care of her child. Living in her house. Driving her car."

Hallie sighed. "Thank you so much for saying that. I needed someone to agree with me today that I have the right to mourn losing myself as well as losing Janet."

"Still no new parents to interview?"

Hallie shook her head. "And I don't expect there will be. We got word from the adoption agency that it doesn't look promising. Plus Ahn's psychologist told us if we didn't find new parents by her third birthday, it would be in her best interest to call off the readoption. Otherwise we'd risk serious emotional damage from another drastic life change."

"How do you feel about that?"

"Do I think it's best for Ahn if Nate and I raise her? No. But we both agree we'll do what we have to do under the circumstances."

"I wasn't going to mention this, Hallie, but George's new boss and his wife have decided to adopt. She told me at the dinner party last week."

"And you like them?"

"Jen and Ben Harris are wonderful people."

"And their names rhyme," Hallie joked.

"I swear you'd like them, Hallie."

Hallie really didn't have any hope that these people would be interested in Ahn, but to humor Liz she said, "Okay. Tell me about them."

"Well, like I said, Ben is George's new boss—CEO for the Boston branch of Allied International Advertising. They transferred here from Los Angeles when Ben got his promotion. Jen isn't working at the moment, but she's a professional fundraiser, and in the past she's worked for organizations like the Make-A-Wish Foundation and the Cystic Fibrosis Foundation. And that's really all I do know about them except that..." Liz paused for a second.

"Sorry, it makes me want to cry every time I think about this. Their first child and their second child were stillborn, Hallie. You can understand why they can't go through that again."

Hallie's heart went out to the couple and she hadn't even met them yet. "Why don't I give you our attorney's number before you leave and you can give it to them? If they're interested, tell them to call Greg's office and set up an interview with us."

Liz beamed at that suggestion. "I would love to do that. For you, for Ahn and for Jen."

"BEN AND JEN. Cute," Nate said while they were eating dinner.

"I made a joke about their names rhyming, too," Hallie told him. "But Liz really likes this couple. She'll have them call Greg, if they're interested."

"Pasta," Ahn demanded from her high chair.

"Pasta, please," Hallie corrected.

Ahn looked directly at Nate.

"Say please," he instructed.

"Please," Ahn said.

Hallie grabbed Ahn's dish, and went to the kitchen for more pasta. But as she did, Nate leaned over and held his hand up.

Ahn slapped his palm with a loud high five.

Hallie frowned at him. "You know how much I hate that, Nate."

"Oops," he said, covering his mouth with his hand.

Ahn burst out laughing.

"No wonder I'm having trouble with her manners. You make a big game out of everything. And I'm sorry, but *please* should *not* be followed by a big high five."

"We're just having fun, Hallie," he said. "Ease up. You're beginning to sound like Roberta."

Hallie felt the blood drain to her feet.

She turned away so she didn't have to look at either of them. She leaned against the counter, reeling from what Nate had said.

She *was* becoming like Roberta. And suddenly Hallie knew why.

Ahn treated Hallie exactly the way she'd treated

Roberta when she'd lost her mother at such an early age. She'd been indifferent toward Roberta and completely defiant because she'd wanted her mother instead of the woman who had taken her place.

Hallie thought back to the one clear memory she did have of her mother. It was the last day Hallie had seen her alive. Roberta had taken her and Janet to the hospital, and her mother had managed to smile at them before she closed her eyes with a weary sigh. Hallie had been too young to understand that her mother would never open her eyes again.

She'd also been to young to understand why Roberta had rushed them into the waiting room and told them to color a nice picture with the crayons and paper she'd taken from Janet's book bag. Hallie had finished her picture first, and when she'd run out into the hallway to show everyone, she remembered being angry because Roberta had her arms around her father.

"We never should have had children," she'd heard her father say as he sobbed against Roberta's shoulder.

"We'll make the best of this, Joe," Roberta assured him. "I promised Val I'd take care of all of you."

In essence, Hallie had lost both of her parents that day. But she didn't realize until now that she'd always blamed Roberta. And that sadly, because of her snotty attitude, Roberta had finally lost patience with her and stopped caring whether Hallie liked her or not.

That was exactly what was beginning to happen between Hallie and Ahn.

Hallie had just lost patience with Ahn over something

as silly as a high five. That made her wonder if maybe she and Roberta would have had a better chance of developing a close relationship if Roberta hadn't given up teaching to take care of her until Hallie was in third grade. Being together day in and day out had fostered more resentment between them. Hallie had refused to do anything Roberta said. And Roberta had been used to children doing *exactly* what she said.

Hallie would not let that happen to her and Ahn.

Nate had told her if they did end up keeping Ahn, she could go back to work and he would stay home until Ahn started school. Did he mean that?

He needed to get a clear idea of what he was signing up for. He'd always helped with Ahn, sure, but she'd been the primary caregiver from the beginning. Nate had always had the freedom to visit his mother when he wanted. Or work on his project when he wanted. Or basically do anything he wanted whenever he wanted.

Mr. Mom was about to get his chance to take over.

HALLIE WAS RIGHT, Nate decided. He did need to be more supportive when it came to Ahn's manners. Unfortunately, Hallie had been in a mood all day.

Hell, who was he kidding?

Lately, Hallie stayed in a mood.

And now Liz had her all pumped up about some couple she knew who just happened to be looking for a child to adopt. How convenient. Maybe they should put pictures of Ahn all over Winchester with a caption that read: Know anyone who might want to adopt this kid?

Liz needed to mind her own damn business.

Especially since he and Hallie had already decided if they couldn't find parents by Ahn's third birthday they would call off the readoption. Nate didn't want anyone stepping in to screw that up.

Nate looked up as Hallie set the replenished bowl in front of Ahn then sat.

"Say thank you."

"Thank you," Ahn said without having to be further prompted.

Nate felt like reaching over and kissing Ahn.

Instead, he stood and walked over to stand behind Hallie's chair. He put his arms around her and bent down to kiss her neck. "I apologize. You're right. I need to give you more support with Ahn's manners. What can I do to make you forgive me for being such an ass?"

She tilted her head up for a kiss.

Nate gave her one.

"Let me go back to work," she said. "Now."

Nate looked down at her. "Now? Seriously?"

"Yes," she said. "You were right, too. I am starting to sound like Roberta, and I don't want to do that to Ahn. Ever. Maybe if we create a break in our schedule, give ourselves some hours apart, she'll be more receptive to me."

"And you're really ready to go back to work full-time?"

"I was thinking only part-time at first. It would give

us a chance to see how you staying home and me working would play out if we do call off the readoption."

Nate knew he couldn't back down now. Not after she mentioned calling off the readoption.

He shrugged. "Sure. I think this is a good idea. Phone your boss tomorrow and see what you can work out."

"And you really wouldn't mind?"

"No. Ahn and I will do fine."

She stood and turned to face him. Her arms slid around his neck as she kissed him. Really kissed him—as though she meant it.

"That's only a sample of how much I appreciate you," she whispered. "Later, you'll get the full entrée."

"I'll hold you to that."

"Then let me give Ahn her bath, and you put the dishes in the dishwasher," she said. "I want to explain to her that I'm going back to work."

Nate nodded okay. But he thought, *What the hell did I just do?*

Of course, he and Ahn would be fine. Nate wasn't worried about that. He was worried about Hallie getting caught up in her career again and coming to the conclusion that if they did call off the readoption he could raise Ahn alone.

Even Nate didn't want that.

Ahn deserved two parents.

Or at least, two parent figures.

But what if once Hallie broke free, she did exactly what he had done when he put his mother in the nursing home? Kept running and never looked back?

After he loaded the dishwasher, Nate climbed the stairs, ready for his nightly ritual of reading twice whatever book Ahn picked. But he paused outside the nursery door, listening as Hallie talked to her while getting Ahn into her pajamas.

"So I want you to be a good girl for Uncle Nate on the days I'm at work, okay? He loves you and he loves me, too, or he wouldn't realize how much I miss the work I do. When you're all grown up, you'll have a career one day. And I don't exactly know how to explain it, sweetie, but there's nothing as rewarding as the satisfaction a person gets from knowing they're the best at what they do. I guess that's why I've been so grumpy lately, and I'm sorry about that. But you and I both know that I don't do my job of taking care of you better than anyone else. I do the best I can, Ahn, but you deserve so much better than I'm able to give you."

Nate stepped away from the door, cursing himself for eavesdropping.

He'd been lying to himself. He'd been so sure that he and Hallie being together meant the three of them would all live happily ever after.

"I'm not the mommy type," she'd said once.

He should have paid more attention to that statement.

NOT ONLY HAD HER BOSS jumped at the chance to have her back, but he'd asked Hallie if she could begin working weekends starting this upcoming one. Hallie didn't hesitate to tell him yes.

Working weekends meant she would still be able to take Ahn to play group on Mondays. She would also be available when Nate went for his weekly visits with his mother. She would still be free for any prospective parent interviews during the week.

Nate, however, hadn't been so thrilled about her working weekends. And he'd seemed downright shocked when she'd told him when she would start.

But Hallie had made mad and passionate love to Nate last night—even more madly and more passionately than usual—as her way of reassuring him that *he* excited her more than work.

Thinking about how much Nate did excite her, Hallie reached out and took his hand. It was Friday pizza night. She would start work tomorrow so they'd celebrated at the pizza parlor. Now they were standing outside the restaurant watching Ahn ride the mechanical pony.

Hallie squeezed Nate's hand. "I'm going to miss you tomorrow."

His laugh had more than a touch of cynicism in it. "I doubt that. You'll be too busy. And you'll love every minute of it."

Hallie didn't like his implication that she was the only one who felt passionate about her work. "The same way you love it when you're out in the field on assignment, you mean?"

"The same way I *loved* it," he stressed. "There are more important things to me now."

Hallie let go of his hand.

Nate had been short with her all day. She'd purposely

ignored him trying to avoid an argument. The last thing she wanted was them at odds when she went to the studio. But now he was being a jerk, and Hallie wasn't putting up with it.

"What's going on with you, Nate? You agreed I could go back to work. But you're acting all pissed about it. If you didn't want me to do this, you should have just told me."

He turned to face her. "I'm not pissed. I'm just concerned."

"Concerned about what?"

"About you becoming so involved in your work again, there won't be any room left in your life for us."

Hallie reached up and kissed him. "There'll always be room for us, Nate. I promise you that."

"I meant Ahn and me, Hallie."

He pushed away from her. But not before she saw the disappointment in his eyes.

"Nate," she called out after him.

He didn't turn around. And he didn't wait for her to catch up. He took Ahn off the horse and headed straight to the Range Rover.

Hallie marched after him. There was just no winning with Nate or Ahn. And Hallie was getting tired of it fast.

He looked over at her. "Why do you put up with me?"

"I was just asking myself that same question."

"I don't blame you," he said. "I've become the king of mixed messages, and I swear, Hallie, my only explanation for why I keep changing my mind is this damn purgatory we're living in. I just want whatever we're doing settled one way or the other. Can you understand that?"

He looked so discouraged Hallie reached out and took his hand. "Yes, I understand that. But we need each other, Nate. If we're going to get through whatever happens with Ahn, we have to stick together."

"That's not what I meant, Hallie. I meant we can settle what happens with Ahn right now. You're already going back to work, and I'm going to stay home with her. That much is settled. Let's settle everything and call off the readoption."

If only she could do that.

"I can't, Nate. I'm sorry. Not when we still have four months left to find the right parents."

"Okay," he said. "We'll do it your way."

"It isn't my way," Hallie said. "It's the right way, Nate. It's what we promised Janet and David we would do when we signed the guardianship agreement."

He didn't answer.

And Hallie didn't push it any further.

HALLIE HAD EXPECTED a skeleton crew on her first day back at the station since it was the weekend. Instead, a big welcome-back party waited for her.

Her boss, Pete Thompson, and almost every employee at the station was there to greet her. The staff lounge had been decorated with a huge banner, balloons were everywhere and an array of fruit and pastries had been brought in for the early morning celebration.

"We can't begin to tell you how much we've missed you, Hallie," Pete said in his speech. "It's good to have you back."

Everyone clapped and cheered.

Five months ago, Hallie wouldn't have been able to handle such a party. But today she reveled in the attention, basked in the glory of knowing how much she'd been missed, and she wasn't going to feel one bit guilty about it.

Here, she was Hallie Weston again, competent executive producer. Here, her opinions mattered and her ability to do her job better than anyone else was admired.

In Winchester she was Janet's poor sister. Ahn's incompetent caregiver. And Nate's…

Unfortunately, at the moment, Hallie wasn't sure what she was to Nate. She'd thought she knew. She'd thought she was his friend, his lover and the person he wanted to share his life with.

But he'd slept with his back to her last night. And she hadn't made things worse by trying to *talk the situation to death,* as he'd once put it. Nate had, however, been in a little bit better mood at breakfast.

He'd kissed her and told her to have a good day when she'd left. He'd even walked her to the car, carrying Ahn and instructing Ahn to wave goodbye. They'd both still been waving as Hallie backed out of the driveway.

As selfish as it was, the second she drove away from Wedge Pond, Hallie's only thought was that finally she was free. Free to be herself. Free to do what she did best. Free to step out of Janet's life and into her own.

She'd called them at home at lunchtime, surprised to get the answering machine. Her call to Nate's cell phone had also gone straight to voice mail. But that really didn't worry Hallie. Nate was forever either forgetting to turn his cell phone on, or leaving it in the house or the car when he did remember to take it with him. The habit was probably a holdover from spending years in remote areas with no cell phone service.

She'd sent him a text message about an hour ago, but she'd yet to get a reply back. It told Hallie Nate was probably still pouting.

She'd lain awake after he'd gone to sleep last night, thinking about all the possibilities their future together could hold if they could find the right parents for Ahn. They could sell the house on Wedge Pond. They could buy one of those great brownstones in Back Bay that would be close to the station so she'd have a short commute.

A brownstone would be perfect for them, not too big, but with enough space to breathe. There would be plenty of room for all of Nate's camera equipment, even a darkroom if he wanted one—he still liked to dabble in black-and-white film. Plus, Ahn would be able to have her own bedroom for times when she came for sleepover visits, which Hallie intended to be often.

When Nate was out of the country on assignment, she could fly to be with him. Or if his location was too dangerous, they could always meet somewhere else to spend a few days together. Hallie could even bring Ahn with her once she was older. What a great opportunity that would be for Ahn to experience different countries and different cultures.

Didn't Nate understand that?

Didn't he understand that they could still be a big part of Ahn's life after the readoption? Did he really not see how much better Ahn's life would be if she had the right parents to raise her?

Hallie propped her elbows on her desk, closed her eyes and reached up to massage her temples. She opened her eyes when she felt the vibration of her cell phone lying next to her on the desk.

Hallie picked up the phone. Nate's text message read:

Been 2 park 4 picnic. C U 2nite. Miss U.

Hallie closed the phone with a sigh.

"I miss you, too, Nate," she said out loud. "Please don't end up making me miss you forever."

HALLIE DIDN'T KNOW what to expect when she arrived home a little before six that evening. This was the first time Nate had taken care of Ahn by himself all day.

She braced herself for the mess she'd probably find, both in the kitchen and in the den. She knew how hard it was to take care of a toddler who was on the run constantly and get anything else done.

Usually it was after dinner while Nate was giving

Ahn her bath before she had time to pick up all of Ahn's toys and get the downstairs in some kind of shape so Gladys wouldn't have a fit. She'd been working with Ahn, teaching her to pick up her toys and put them into the box beside the fireplace. That usually resulted in Ahn taking more toys out than she was putting in.

But when Hallie walked into the den, the mess she'd expected wasn't there. The room was toy-free, clear and neat.

"I'm home," she called out, walking toward the kitchen, another area that was also relatively tidy.

She smiled when Nate walked out of the dining room.

He held out his arms and Hallie walked into them.

"Where's Ahn?" Hallie asked, kissing him.

"Already in her high chair," he said. "We were waiting for you."

Hallie accepted a kiss back. "Everything looks great around here. I'm extremely impressed."

"Thanks," he said and kissed her again. "Want to go up and change first?"

"No," Hallie said. "Just let me wash my hands."

Hallie kicked off her heels and padded barefoot toward the bathroom off the kitchen. "I'll be there to kiss you in a minute, sweet girl," Hallie called to Ahn.

She was even more impressed when she walked into the dining room a few minutes later.

"Wow," Hallie said. "Candlelight *and* the good china? What did I do to deserve this?"

That was when Hallie saw the dog.

A big black dog. A big black dog sitting beside Ahn's high chair as if he belonged there.

Hallie's gaze cut to Nate.

"The Humane Society was at the park when Ahn and I went on our picnic. The minute Ahn saw him, she pointed and said, 'Buster.'"

Buster was the black Lab in Ahn's favorite book.

"That's your explanation? Ahn pointed to a dog, so you walked over and adopted it and brought him home? If she'd pointed to an elephant and said, 'Toby,' would you have brought it home, too?"

Toby was the elephant in Ahn's second-favorite book.

"I thought you were real big on adoption, Hallie."

So that was it.

The dog was her payback.

"I am, Nate. Completely."

"Then you shouldn't have a problem with Buster."

"Did you even stop to think the dog might hurt her, Nate? You don't know this dog's temperament."

"I'm not stupid, Hallie. He's a retired service dog, okay? The old man he was assigned to died, and the family didn't want him. That's how he ended up for adoption."

Hallie wasn't convinced. "But couldn't they have assigned him to someone else? I know dogs like him are expensive."

Nate shook his head. "He's at the age where they

consider him too old to reassign. He's paid his dues. It's time he simply enjoyed life."

Hallie looked at the dog. He was staring at her expectantly, his tail wagging slightly as if he knew exactly what was going on. Ahn leaned down and fed him a piece of pasta. His tail wagged again.

Hallie looked back at Nate. "And what do you intend to do with him *later?*"

And Nate knew exactly what *later* meant.

"If *later* happens," he said, "that's when I'll worry about it."

He pulled out her chair and Hallie walked over to it.

Their relationship was quickly beginning to unravel at the seams. And short of calling off the readoption, there was nothing Hallie could do to stop it.

NATE REACHED OVER and turned off the light. Tonight, Hallie rolled over with *her* back to him. Staring at the baby monitor screen on her bedside table reminded her why.

Ahn was fast asleep in the new trundle bed they'd purchased when she'd fallen out of her crib climbing over the railing. And a now clean Buster was stretched out on the sheets of the pulled-out bottom mattress.

She might have lost the argument about keeping the dog, but not without establishing some rules—the first of which was the bath Nate and Ahn had given him immediately after dinner. She'd also made certain that Nate knew it was his responsibility to feed and take care of the dog. And the first time he peed or pooped in the house, chewed up anything or showed any sign that he wasn't tolerant of a two-year-old, he was out of there.

It wasn't that she didn't like the dog. He'd immediately won her over with his big, sad eyes. But Buster was one more nail Nate was constantly driving into the readoption coffin. Instead of making after-adoption plans for their futures—three of them—he was sticking his head in the sand, pretending the readoption wasn't going to happen.

And maybe it wouldn't.

Hallie was prepared for that possibility. If those were the cards dealt to them, she would make the best of it. But Ahn deserved better than being raised by two people who were trying to make the best of it. Hallie had lived that life with her father and Roberta.

She was still staring at a sleeping Ahn and her new roommate when Nate's arm slid around her waist, pulling her against him. Hallie told herself to push him away and send him a message that she didn't appreciate him blindsiding her with the dog. He could have called first. Of course he hadn't—he'd known exactly what her answer would have been.

He nuzzled against her neck, taking the tiny bites that he knew drove her crazy. And when he nibbled at her ear, Hallie could already feel herself caving.

"I should have called you about the dog," he said.

"Yes, you should have," Hallie told him, but she was

already thinking how withholding sex as punishment had always seemed petty to her.

So they'd had an argument. That didn't mean she didn't still love him and want his body. All Nate had to do was touch her to set her on fire.

Like now.

His hand moved up to cup her breast, his thumb exploring her nipple. Hallie bit down on her lower lip. The sensation was delicious.

"And I shouldn't have pressed you last night to call off the readoption."

"No," Hallie agreed. "You shouldn't have."

They were nude.

They always slept nude.

She could feel him growing harder as he pressed against her. He ran his tongue along her shoulder, and Hallie shivered at the sensation.

"But most of all, I should have made love to you last night the way I want to make love to you right now."

When his hand moved downward Hallie rolled over on her back, finally giving him full access to what he was seeking. He toyed with her, just as she knew he would, taking turns with his fingers and his mouth as he pleasured her, getting her ready for what she really wanted. And what she really wanted was Nate deep inside her, driving into her, showing her how much he wanted her.

She whispered his name.

He was giving her what she wanted now.

So deep inside her she was already coming.

And Nate would make her come again.
Several times before the night was over.
The way Nate always did.

CHAPTER FOURTEEN

IF HALLIE HAD KNOWN how much easier Buster was going to make her life, she would have searched the animal shelter for a service dog months ago. The dog was amazing.

She no longer had to watch Ahn every second. Any time Ahn headed for the deck steps or tried to climb up the stairs to the second floor, Buster would get in front of her, blocking her way.

"Move, Buster," Ahn would order.

Buster would lick her face, but he wouldn't let her pass.

Letting the dog sleep in Ahn's room had also turned out to be a godsend, even though Hallie had had her doubts at first. Ahn had never slept completely throughout the night, and Hallie had worried the dog would disturb her. She couldn't count the number of times the monitor would come to life and she would hear Ahn whimper, not waking fully, but on the verge. Hallie would go in and adjust her covers, rub her back for a few minutes, and Ahn would be fast asleep again.

Since Buster's arrival, Ahn had slept peacefully all through the night. It could have only been a coincidence—Ahn was, after all, getting older. But Hallie believed Ahn felt safe knowing the dog was sleeping on the lower mattress.

So Ahn and Buster were good.

Things had even been getting better between her and Nate, though Hallie knew his improved attitude was only because it was October and they still didn't have a single couple to interview. She'd reminded Nate last night that she *would* go back to work full-time in February. He'd assured her if that was what she decided to do he was still okay with staying home.

Problem solved, as he liked to say.

But for whom?

Certainly not for Ahn.

Hallie walked into the laundry room with a basket of dirty clothes to leave for Gladys tomorrow morning. Tuesday was laundry day, and Hallie didn't dare forget it since Gladys had politely reminded her of that before she left thirty minutes ago.

Hallie paused when the phone rang.

But when Nate yelled out from the kitchen that he would get the phone, she went about her business, carefully separating the clothes into the appropriate baskets lined up on the counter the way Gladys preferred. When she walked out of the laundry room and into the kitchen, however, Nate was standing by the kitchen bar, a frown on his face and his hands at his waist.

Hallie raised an eyebrow in question. "What?"

"Jen and Ben, that's what." He swore.

"Nate!" Hallie scolded.

She quickly looked around for Ahn, who was sitting on the floor in the den. Thankfully, she was too engrossed in lining blocks along Buster's back to pay attention to Nate's cursing.

Hallie looked back at him. "Does that mean we have an interview?"

"You tell me, Hallie," he snapped. "Do you really see the need to interview these people?"

"Absolutely."

"Well, that's just great," he said, almost shouting now. "The interview's at two o'clock tomorrow. I hope you and Liz Foster are happy."

He walked into the den and picked up Ahn. Then he stormed out the French doors to the deck. Buster stood, shook the blocks off his back, then lumbered after them.

Hallie slowly counted to ten. And then she counted to ten all over again. How could you love someone so much and still want to strangle him?

Shaking her head, Hallie walked over to close the door. And that was when she heard the car door slam.

"Dammit!" she swore, hurrying toward the steps.

When Hallie rounded the corner of the house she could see that Ahn was already strapped into the car seat while Buster leaped in beside her. After shutting that door Nate jerked the driver's-side door open.

Hallie put her hands on her hips. "Will you at least tell me where you're taking her?"

He glared at her. "What do you care as long as she's

gone? You've made it clear you can't wait to give her away." He revved the engine to life and drove away.

Hallie was left wounded. Not just from Nate's cruel accusation, but also from the cold, hard look in his eyes.

FUNNY HOW THE ONLY PLACE where Nate wanted to go was to see his mother. His mother wouldn't remember Ahn, of course. And she wouldn't even remember they had been there. But Nate had a bad feeling if he didn't take Ahn to see his mother now, he might not have that chance.

Greg had raved about Jen and Ben Harris. He'd even said he was absolutely certain that these were the perfect parents for Ahn. He was sure Nate and Hallie already agreed since Hallie's friend had been responsible for having the Harrises get in touch with him.

That had really pissed Nate off.

As if Nate should agree on Liz Foster's say-so. But with Greg and Liz both singing this couple's praises, Hallie would be falling all over herself in agreement. That would leave Nate the odd man out and looking like a selfish prick if he found something wrong with them.

When they reached the nursing home, Nate parked and hit the power window buttons. He told Buster to stay and took Ahn out of her car seat.

It took fifteen minutes before they finally got away from the nurses' desk. All of the nurses had to take turns playing with Ahn and telling Nate how adorable she was and how much she'd grown since they'd last seen her.

Finally, they made their way down the long corridor toward his mother's room. And Nate prayed with every step he took that she would be sitting in her wheelchair today instead of in bed.

On the days when he did find her in bed, rolled over on her side, staring hopelessly at the blank wall, the memories were so painful Nate couldn't force himself to stay. But when she was sitting up, even if it was only his imagination, every now and then she would look at Nate as if she remembered him.

When he pushed the door open and walked inside, he was relieved to see his mother in her wheelchair. But to Nate's surprise she wasn't alone.

Nate walked up beside her and put Ahn down. "Hi, Mom." He looked over at the elderly woman sitting in the wheelchair beside her. "Who's your friend?"

Her new friend had snow-white hair and bright blue eyes, and the twinkle in them told Nate that unlike his mother, this woman was in full possession of her faculties. She smiled up at him and said, "I'm Rose from Room 419. I watch the birds with your mother sometimes. She doesn't seem to mind."

Nate smiled back at her. "I'm sure she enjoys your company, Rose."

"Well, hello there," Rose said to Ahn, who had walked over to her, suddenly fascinated with the rabbit's foot on the keychain lying on Rose's lap. Rose picked up the keys and handed them to Ahn to play with. "Is this your little girl?"

"Yes." In that moment, Nate knew it was true. In his heart Ahn felt like his little girl now.

How could he possibly give her up? Yet, at the same time, how could he possibly keep Ahn if Jen and Ben Harris really were the perfect parents for her?

He'd proven he could take care of Ahn on the weekends. But what about after Hallie went back to work full-time? He'd talked to Dirk last week and in a few months he would be expected to do his part promoting the documentary. What was he going to do with Ahn then? Tell Hallie she needed to take another leave of absence until his promotional tour was over?

No, Ahn would end up with a nanny.

And that truth hit Nate hard.

He'd told Hallie once that all they really had to offer Ahn was finding the best possible parents to raise her. And as much as it hurt Nate to admit it, he and Hallie were not the best possible parents. He'd lost sight of that somewhere along the way.

"What's your name?" Rose asked, looking down at Ahn, who was still fascinated by the rabbit's foot.

"Her name is Ahn," Nate told Rose. "And she's actually my niece. I've been taking care of her for my brother."

That truth was even harder for Nate to face.

He'd been substituting Ahn in place of David. Trying to hold on to that one last connection he had to his brother. But it was time to let David go now. And if the

Harrises turned out to be the right parents, he had to let Ahn go, too.

But did he have the courage to go through with it?

NATE HAD BEEN GONE so long that Hallie was getting worried. So worried, in fact, she resorted to calling Roberta, even though Hallie had little desire to broadcast the problems she and Nate were having.

"Why, no, Hallie. Nate and Ahn aren't here. Are they supposed to be?"

"I don't know where they are, Roberta. Greg called to say he'd scheduled an interview with that couple Liz told me about for two o'clock tomorrow. I was hoping Nate had gone to ask you to babysit."

"Of course I'll babysit. Have you tried Nate's cell?"

"His phone is sitting right here on the counter. It makes me absolutely crazy when he does that. What's the purpose of having a damn cell phone if you never have it on and never take it with you?"

"Okay," Roberta said. "What *aren't* you telling me?"

"We had an argument about the interview. I think we should meet the couple. And Nate, of course, doesn't." So much for not broadcasting their problems. But Hallie was so frustrated, it felt better letting the whole thing out.

"You had to see this coming, Hallie. I warned you not to give Nate false hopes by letting him think you were keeping Ahn."

"I wasn't giving him false hopes, Roberta. We had to discuss what we were going to do if we didn't find new parents. Never once did I lead him to believe I wouldn't want to interview anyone else."

"But in Nate's mind, Ahn already has parents, Hallie. That's the problem."

Hallie groaned. "God, this is such a mess. It's been a mess from day one."

"Well, regardless of the argument, you know Nate wouldn't do anything stupid."

"Does the name Buster ring a bell?"

"Now, Hallie. You love that dog, too."

"How long should I wait for them to come back before I panic and go out looking?"

"How long have they been gone?"

"About an hour."

"Don't worry, I'm sure they'll be home soon."

"You might have to come get me out of jail later," Hallie said. "I'm angry enough to throttle Nate right now."

"Focus instead on calming down, and stay calm when they get home. Shouting at each other won't solve a thing. The Colonel and I will come out first thing in the morning and stay with Ahn."

They said their goodbyes and hung up. Hallie took the phone outside and sat at the patio table to wait.

She was furious with Nate. Yet, she was worried about him, too.

She'd depended on him too much right from the start. She'd let him bear the burden of all the funeral and legal arrangements, taking her own time to grieve without giving him the same opportunity. And the worst thing she'd done was talk him into helping her take care of Ahn.

Now Nate was paying the consequences.

Hallie wiped away a tear.

It only made sense that Nate would see the readoption as another loss. If he let go of Ahn, he'd have to let go of David, too. Why had it taken her so long to figure that out? How could he ever forgive her because she hadn't?

When she heard the car pull up in the driveway, Hallie forced herself not to get up. Roberta was right. Starting another shouting match wouldn't solve anything. Besides, at the moment all Hallie wanted to do was fall on her knees and beg Nate's forgiveness.

Buster came around the corner first, followed by Nate, who carried Ahn.

When he put her down on the deck she ran straight to Hallie. Hallie picked her up for a hug that lasted only a second before Ahn squirmed out of Hallie's arms and ran to her sandbox.

"Can we talk now?" Hallie asked.

"If I can go first," he said and sat beside her. "I should have told you where I was going. I took Ahn to see my mother."

Hallie reached over to clasp his hand. That had to have been hard for him.

"I took her because Greg told me he was certain that these people are the right parents." He swallowed. "I started a fight with you because that's the last thing I wanted to hear. I know we owe it to Ahn to see if Greg's right. And if they are the best parents for her, Hallie, I give you my word—you won't have any problem from me."

Hallie planted a kiss on his fingers. "All I've ever wanted for Ahn was the best parents, Nate. I don't want to give her away. I want to give her the brightest future possible."

"I know that," he said. "And I want that, too. I won't let my own selfish reasons stand in the way again."

Hallie squeezed his hand. "I was just thinking how selfish I've been, too. Pushing you into helping me take care of Ahn. Pushing you into my bed. Pushing you to continue with the readoption even when I knew you were having serious doubts. Can you forgive me for not understanding how hard all of this has been on you?"

"I made my own choices, Hallie. There's nothing to forgive. I love you. And I've never had any doubts about that."

It was the first time he'd said those words out loud.

Nate had shown her in a thousand different ways that he loved her, but he'd never said it. Hallie had held back, too. He'd told her from the beginning that he couldn't promise her forever. She hadn't wanted him to think she'd forgotten that.

"I love you, too, Nate" Hallie said. "I always have."

Regardless of what the future held, for this moment what they had was enough.

HALLIE ROLLED OVER and snuggled against him. Nate pulled the sheet up around her shoulders and waited until the sound of her even breathing told him she had fallen asleep. He'd been lying awake for hours, his stomach in knots over the interview tomorrow.

But he'd given Hallie his word, and he wouldn't go back on it.

She'd told him she'd been selfish. But so had he. He'd selfishly pushed Hallie into a role she didn't want. She wanted to be Ahn's aunt. It had never been her choice to be Ahn's mother.

They'd talked a long time after they'd made love. She shared her visions for their future if the Harris couple turned out okay. How involved she and Nate could be in Ahn's life. How they could move back to the city and buy a brownstone where Ahn could have her own bedroom and stay over on a regular basis.

She'd assumed he would eventually pick up overseas assignments after he finished the documentary. She'd even talked about flying to meet him and bringing Ahn when she got older. Nate wasn't sure why he'd let her assume that, other than the fact that she was only speculating, rather than them committing to any concrete plans.

His assignment days were over. He had too much to lose now.

Before Hallie and Ahn became a part of his life, he'd had nothing to lose. No attachments. No reason to avoid putting himself in harm's way. His mother hadn't even known he was alive, and David hadn't counted.

Not because Nate didn't love his brother, but because David had his own family that always came first.

Family first.

Nate squeezed his eyes shut against an instant flashback: him standing rigid over his father's casket, holding David's hand, his arm around his mother's waist to help keep her standing. He'd hated his father that day. Hated that everyone called him a hero. Hated the fire chief giving the eulogy, saying, "William Brock was an honorable captain who always put his squadron first."

"What about family first?" Nate had wanted to yell.

He opened his eyes, shaking off that memory.

Regardless of what happened after tomorrow's interview, Ahn and Hallie would always be his family. As for what the future held...

He loved Hallie. And he loved Ahn. That much he knew.

But he still had a lot of things to figure out about himself.

CHAPTER FIFTEEN

HALLIE COULD TELL Nate was as nervous as she was waiting in Greg's office. Greg finally walked through the door with a folder in his hand.

He propped a hip on the corner of his desk. "When the Harrises contacted me directly I decided to bypass the adoption agency and interview them personally due to the time crunch we're in. If you like them and decide to move forward, I'll have a complete background and criminal check run on them."

He held up the folder. "I made a few notes during my interview if you want me to go over them."

Nate stood. "That won't be necessary. Let's just get this over with."

Hallie didn't disagree.

She headed for the door with Nate. They both knew the personal interview would tell the real story. Hallie just prayed Nate would give them a chance. He'd been stoic all day, but Hallie still suspected underneath his calm exterior there was a bubbling volcano ready to erupt at any minute.

She said a silent prayer that wouldn't happen.

Hallie could already see the couple through the glass

walls of the boardroom as Greg escorted them down the hallway, but their backs were to her. She glanced at Nate one last time before they reached the boardroom. He still had the same impassive look on his face.

Hallie would take impassive.

Jen turned around when they entered.

"From the shocked looks on your faces I assume no one told you I was Vietnamese," Jen said.

"No," Hallie finally said. "We had no idea."

Jen smiled. "What a shame. I was hoping to use that to my advantage."

Hallie liked her immediately.

"Thank you, honey," Ben said, putting his arm around her, "for showing these nice people how incredibly tactful you *aren't*."

Everyone laughed, including Nate. Hallie began to relax a little.

Even Nate couldn't deny that Ben and Jen were a striking couple. Ben was as handsome as Jen was pretty, both dressed stylishly. Everything about them said successful, polished and educated.

Greg made the formal introductions then left them alone to get acquainted. Nate and Ben did the obligatory handshake, but Jen had Hallie in a hug before Hallie saw it coming.

"I'm so sorry about your sister and your brother-in-law," Jen said when she stepped back.

"I'm sorry for your loss, as well," Hallie told her.

"Thank you," Jen said and nodded toward the guys.

"I just heard Ben say something about the Red Sox. That'll be a thirty-minute conversation."

"Maybe longer," Hallie said. "Nate's a big Red Sox fan, too."

"Let's go over there," Jen said.

They sat at the far end of the table. Jen took both of Hallie's hands in her own.

"Now," she said, "tell me all about Ahn."

Hallie hadn't felt this close to a woman since Janet.

"She's amazing," Hallie said. "She's had some developmental issues due to the time she spent in the orphanage, but she's extremely bright and the extra time Nate and I have been able to spend with her has helped her overcome most of those problems. Our goal right now is potty training. She's doing better than I expected, and she wears pull-ups during the day, but we're not quite there yet. Her speech is improving every day and she's walking—no, running well. She already knows her colors and she's learning the alphabet and her numbers. When Janet and David first adopted her she didn't engage with people. She's doing much better with the adults she sees regularly. With other children Ahn is up and down. Sometimes she plays with them, sometimes not. But at least she acknowledges their presence, even if she doesn't share or join them.

"She'll be three in February, and, according to the psychologist we've been working with, she's finally catching up with children her age."

Hallie pulled a picture from her purse. Ahn in her

sandbox grinning for the camera. "Nate took this yesterday."

Hallie watched Jen's expression as she studied the picture. Janet's *a sudden rush of joy* came to mind.

"She's gorgeous," Jen said, looking at Hallie as she handed her the picture.

"Believe me, she knows it," Hallie said. "She's quite the little diva. And she's a shameless flirt."

"My kind of woman," Jen said.

They both laughed.

Jen's expression turned serious. "I can tell you're crazy about Ahn, Hallie. So I'm going to ask the obvious. Why the adoption?"

"I want Ahn to have the type of mother she had in Janet. A mother who puts being a mother above anything or anyone else. Who is one hundred percent certain she wants to be a parent. And who is happy with herself for making that decision."

"And you aren't a Janet," Jen said.

"No," Hallie said. "I'm not a Janet."

Jen smiled. "Good news. I am."

"What else should I know about you?"

"Well, I'm originally from New York and my parents came to the U.S. after the fall of Saigon at the end of the Vietnam War. They scrimped and saved and opened the restaurant they still run in Brooklyn. All five of us kids were born here. I'm the middle child. I have two older brothers and two younger sisters and my parents made sure we all had college educations." She paused before she said, "I guess the point I'm trying to make is that I have a large, loving family to share with Ahn, Hallie, and they would welcome her with open arms the same way they would welcome you and Nate."

What a blessing that would be to have a large family.

"How did you meet Ben?"

Jen glanced across the room at Ben and smiled. The love she felt was evident.

"Ben's father introduced us, actually. I was in New Jersey working on Senator Harris's fundraising committee and he dropped by our campaign headquarters for a visit. He was immediately impressed with me, of course." She laughed at that. "And he told me I was the most delightful young woman he'd met in a long time and that he would like to introduce me to his son. I didn't realize he meant right then. But the next thing I knew, he was motioning Ben over. I fell in love instantly." Jen looked up. "And here Ben is walking in our direction now."

"Time to switch," Ben said, smiling at Hallie. "Nate and I have already solved all of the Red Sox lineup problems."

He sat beside Hallie.

"May I?" he asked, pointing to the picture Hallie was still holding.

Hallie studied Ben's expression. Wistful maybe?

He handed the picture back to Hallie. "Our first daughter would have been five next month. And our second daughter would have been the age Ahn is now. Nate asked me if I was ready to become a father, so I'll tell you what I told him. I'm already a father. I already know what it's like to have a father's hopes and dreams for his little girls. And I know the type of love only a parent can feel for a child. All I'm hoping for right now is a chance for Jen and me to meet Ahn. But you have my promise that if we do bond with Ahn and we are lucky enough to have her as our daughter, she will be loved, and cared for, and treasured the same way our own precious daughters would have been."

Hallie reached out and touched Ben's arm, but the words were stuck in her throat.

He patted Hallie's hand, as if to say he understood.

NATE HADN'T EXPECTED to like Ben. But he did. Ben was a straight-up guy who didn't dodge questions and looked him straight in the eye. He'd sized Ben up in a matter of seconds. But Jen was a different story.

Nate could tell she was sizing him up, yet nothing about her put him on the defensive. She didn't seem pretentious. Nor did she appear to be judgmental.

Genuine.

Yeah, that was the word he would use to describe her.

"Hallie explained why she feels adoption is the right choice for Ahn," she said. "Would you mind telling me how you feel about it?"

Nate refused to lie about it. "Truthfully, I'm not convinced adoption is the best choice for Ahn. I'm still struggling with that. But I want whatever situation is going to help her live up to her potential. That's why I'm here. I owe it to Ahn to meet you."

He couldn't tell if she liked his answer.

"I appreciate your honesty. And I'll be honest with you. Ben and I have our concerns about Ahn's age. When we decided to adopt, we had an infant in mind."

"I can understand that," Nate said. "Ahn's age is a big factor for us, too. Uprooting her again could have serious consequences if we wait much longer. That's a large part of my concern."

"I agree. This is an important decision for all of us. There's no room for mistakes where a child's future is concerned."

No room for mistakes. Nate couldn't have said it better.

Jen smiled at him. "Ahn is extremely fortunate to have you and Hallie, Nate. It takes exceptional people to assume responsibility for children. Regardless of whether we move forward after today, I want you to know I admire you both."

"Thank you" seemed inadequate but it was all Nate could think to say.

As Ben and Hallie approached, Nate didn't have to wonder if Hallie thought Jen and Ben were also exceptional people. He could see it on her face.

Hallie had asked him to keep an open mind. To do the right thing for Ahn.

Ben and Jen could very well be the right thing.

"THAT WAS THE SHOCK of a lifetime," Hallie told Nate as soon as they left Greg's office. "I still can't believe Liz or Greg didn't mention Jen was Vietnamese."

"There was no reason for them to mention it," he said. "It shouldn't matter."

"But it really does matter when you think about it, Nate. Don't you realize how important it would be to Ahn to have the opportunity to be exposed to her own culture? To actually have Vietnamese family of her own?"

"It's something to consider. But I don't think Jen being Vietnamese should automatically make her the best mother for Ahn."

"You know I can't stop thinking about what they've been through losing two babies. You'll probably think I'm crazy but it's almost as if Janet has a hand in this. Look at the coincidences. Ben just happens to be transferred here to Boston and is George Foster's boss. And Liz just happens to have been one of Janet's closest friends." Hallie shivered. "I swear the cosmos is at work here."

She reached for his hand as they left the office building and walked toward the parking garage. "And I found Jen's story absolutely amazing. Her parents coming to New York with nothing after the fall of Saigon. Saving to buy their own business. Raising five kids and putting them all through college. It's the epitome of the American dream and the exact kind of story I'd love to produce for an unsung heroes segment for the station."

"I would have thought you'd be more interested in producing a segment on Ben's wealthy father."

"Very funny," Hallie said, bumping him with her hip.

"Are you kidding me? You'd turn down an interview with a Republican senator? I don't think so."

Hallie laughed. "And wouldn't Janet and David throw a fit if they knew *you* sold them out and agreed to interview Republicans as potential parents."

"You've never fooled me about your politics, Hallie. You've pretended to be conservative all these years to piss me off and get me to argue with you."

Hallie leaned in and kissed him as he opened the door of the SUV for her. "I guess you'll never know for sure, will you?"

She was so relieved Nate wasn't in a gloomy mood after the interview. And she'd been thrilled when Nate had been the one to invite Ben and Jen to dinner on Friday night so they could meet Ahn and get to know each other in a less formal setting.

For the first time since the accident, she was beginning to feel as if everything would be okay. For Ahn. For her and Nate. Even for Jen and Ben. They'd all been through so much. How appropriate if they ended up together as one family.

If Friday night went well, she would ask for a home visit to see where Ahn might be living. And if that proved successful...

Hallie suddenly turned sideways in her seat, realizing for the first time Nate simply sat there, hands on the steering wheel, staring straight ahead. He finally looked over at her.

"They're the right parents, aren't they?"

Hallie didn't lie to him. "Yes," she said. "I think they are."

"And if I need some space after Ahn is settled?"

Hallie felt the crack zigzag through her heart. She faced forward again.

"I won't beg you to stay, Nate. But I can't promise I will *wait* for you forever."

He said, "Then promise not to hate me when I go."

HALLIE SAT ON THE SIDE of the bed, staring at the monitor. Nate, Ahn and Buster were all piled up together on Ahn's bed while Nate read the bedtime story.

They hadn't had the opportunity to talk once they returned to Wedge Pond after the interview with Ben and Jen because Roberta and The Colonel had stayed for dinner.

How Hallie made it through dinner without falling apart, she didn't know. But as the minutes passed and Nate's request continued to echo in her head, a deadly calm settled over her.

It wasn't until Nate launched their nightly routine— giving Ahn her bath and a snack, reading stories— that Hallie finally sat down with the bomb Nate had dropped.

Was she heartbroken that he didn't plan to stick around if the readoption happened?

Yes.

Would she survive?

Yes.

She could understand why Nate was confused about

what they should or shouldn't do where Ahn was concerned. And she could understand why he wasn't sure about what he did or didn't want. Their lives had been turned upside down from the moment that impaired driver crossed the median. This situation had been tearing them apart little by little, day after day. None of it had been their fault. And, more importantly, very little of it had been their choosing.

But it would be her fault if Hallie didn't tell Nate exactly how she felt. No what-ifs. No maybes. No miscommunications. Nothing but the truth.

She watched the monitor until Nate turned off Ahn's light. When he walked into the bedroom, Hallie patted the vacant place on the bed beside her.

He had to notice, of course, that she was still fully dressed, not waiting for him in bed as usual. And she knew his glance toward the foot of the bed meant he didn't miss the basket filled with his clothes that she'd neatly folded and had waiting for him.

Nate walked over and sat beside her. His resigned expression said he'd seen this coming.

"I could never hate you," Hallie told him. "I love you. I love you enough to let you go, the same way I love Ahn enough to let her go. But I deserve better. I deserve to be loved by a man who has no doubt that my face is the first thing he wants to see when he wakes up and the last thing he wants to see before he goes to sleep. The fact that you feel the need to leave tells me you're not sure you feel that way about me. Unless that changes, Nate, the only thing I'll ever have to offer you is the friendship I hope we'll still have when all of this is over."

Nate reached out and caressed the side of her face. He kissed her, then left, taking the basket with him.

The sound of the door gently closing was Hallie's signal to fall apart.

NATE STAYED BEHIND THE camera most of Friday night, where he was safe, and where his only task was to capture what was right in front of him. Surprisingly, what was right in front of him warmed his heart.

The images he caught were the equivalent of a Rockwell painting and a Hallmark commercial all rolled into one. With every picture, he was newly amazed at how easily Ahn warmed up to Jen and to Ben.

They both sat on the floor with Ahn, who showed off stacking her building blocks higher and higher. She let out a delighted squeal when they tumbled to the floor, her favorite part of the whole game.

Snap—Ben helping Ahn pick up the blocks.

Snap—Jen clapping her hands in approval.

Snap—Hallie looking on and smiling.

Nate lowered the camera when Hallie looked directly at him. They exchanged a poignant smile.

She'd been right to ask him to leave her bed. She'd also been right about deserving better. He'd give anything if he could be that man she deserved with no doubts whatsoever. But he couldn't.

Not now.

Maybe never.

She approached him. "Can I talk to you outside a minute?"

Nate nodded and followed her outside on the deck. Although they hadn't said much to each other since Tuesday night, there hadn't been any animosity. They'd simply gone through their daily routines as usual, giving each other time to get used to the distance.

She leaned against the railing. The October night had a chill to it. Nate took off the shirt he was wearing over his T-shirt and put it around her shoulders.

She thanked him, then said, "I made the decision a long time ago that when we found new parents for Ahn, I would sign over my half of the house to you. I think we both already know we've found them."

"I agree," Nate said. "The three of them will make a great family. But I don't want this house. I want us to sell it. And I want you to use the proceeds to buy the brownstone you talked about so Ahn can have her own bedroom. Will you do that for me?"

She looked over at him. "If that's what you really want, then yes, I will buy the brownstone. But what about you? What are your plans, now?"

"I'm going to California."

"Your documentary?"

Nate nodded.

"Funny you should mention selling the house," she said. "Jen mentioned earlier that this was exactly the type of home they've been trying to find. They're still living in a condo they've been renting."

"That would be perfect for Ahn," Nate said, already

following Hallie's reason for mentioning it. "She wouldn't be uprooted."

"Jen has also invited us to go to New York next week so we can meet her family. Ben's parents are coming, too."

She didn't say it specifically but he could hear the doubt in her tone, the question whether he'd join them.

"I wouldn't miss it," Nate said.

Hallie handed his shirt over, then went inside. Nate remained where he was for a long time.

He would go to New York for Ahn and for Hallie. But after that, he was done.

When he left New York, it would not be to come back to Wedge Pond. Ahn had new parents now. There wasn't any reason to drag out the inevitable, and they didn't need him to help sort out the details of the adoption and house sale. Hallie was perfectly capable of making all of the arrangements.

As for him, he could load everything he owned into the Ranger Rover—his clothes, his cameras, all of it—and start driving west. Anything he needed to sign they could courier to him.

Including the adoption papers.

Especially the adoption papers.

Nate couldn't be here for that.

CHAPTER SIXTEEN

IT HAD BEEN SIX MONTHS since Nate had left for California. Every day that passed mocked Hallie. He obviously wasn't coming back. Most days she missed him so badly she regretted not begging him to stay. And then there were days like today when she was at peace with her decision to let him go.

Life did, after all, go on.

On days like today Hallie focused on the things she *did* have to be thankful for in spite of Nate's absence. As always, Ahn was at the center of everything that made her grateful and made her happy.

Hallie walked to the refrigerator, but paused as she took in the paper that decorated the door. She smiled at the latest picture Ahn had drawn in preschool.

Ahn had printed her name in big letters over the stick figure of a little girl with a huge smile on her face. And over a stick figure dog she'd printed "Buster" with the *S* turned backward. According to Jen, the teacher claimed Ahn was well ahead of the other children in her class.

Hallie smiled at that thought, too.

She opened the refrigerator and grabbed a bottled water before she returned to the kitchen table, where she had dozens of photographs—most of them photos that Nate had taken—separated into sections. Now that she had the pictures sorted, she was ready to put them into an album she was making for Ahn.

Hallie took her memory-keeping role seriously.

The first picture she picked up tugged at Hallie's heartstrings. Nate had taken it the day the two of them met Janet and David at the airport when they'd first brought Ahn home.

Hallie slid the photo into place and reached for another. Ahn's Christening. Janet was holding Ahn, David had his arm around Janet's shoulder and both of them were looking down at Ahn with so much love.

Hallie continued inserting pictures. Ahn at the pizza place with tomato sauce all over her face. Roberta holding Ahn, both of them looking up at the Fourth of July fireworks. Ahn feeding the ducks. Ahn sneaking Buster pasta from her high chair. Ahn in her sandbox. Ahn in the bathtub, wearing a hat made of bubbles. Ahn and Nate asleep on the sofa, Ahn curled up in the crook of his arm.

Hallie reached for the next stack.

She smiled when she picked up the picture of Ahn feeding the pigeons in Central Park when they'd all gone to New York to meet Jen's and Ben's families for the first time. The next one was of Ahn sitting between Jen's extremely gracious and wonderful parents. Senator Harris holding Ahn, Ben's mother smiling brightly for the camera. There was a group shot with everyone—

Ahn's new parents, her grandparents, her cousins and all of her aunts and uncles, including Nate and Hallie.

In the next stack was a picture of Ahn, sitting on Katharine's lap. Hallie had taken it shortly after the readoption. With Nate in California, she'd promised she'd visit Katharine often. Nate called to check on his mother regularly, but Hallie knew he appreciated her going.

The next picture was of Ahn standing in the middle of her new bedroom shortly after Hallie bought the brownstone in Back Bay. Ahn in Hallie's back court-yard with Buster, who ended up living with Hallie due to Ben's allergies. Ahn and Buster curled up together, asleep on the sofa in Hallie's den.

Next were holiday pictures—the first Thanksgiving and Christmas after the accident. Hallie had thought so many times how much more difficult last year's holidays would have been without Jen and Ben. The only thing that could have made the season better would have been if Nate had flown in to celebrate with them.

She laughed at the first picture in the stack. Ahn had a huge turkey leg on her chair tray—Buster looking up expectantly at it. Roberta and The Colonel holding up their wineglasses in a toast. Jen and Ben kissing at the table.

There was a picture of Ahn sitting in front of the Christmas tree, frantically tearing open presents, Hallie, Ben and Jen looking at her adoringly. Ahn opening Nate's present from California—a new edition of her favorite Toby the elephant books.

The last holiday picture was Hallie's favorite—Ahn asleep on Hallie's lap, her sweet head resting against Hallie's shoulder. The adults had all been sitting around the table talking after dinner and Ahn had suddenly walked over to Hallie and held up her arms.

"Hold me, Aunt Hallie." Seconds later, she was fast asleep. Ahn reaching out to her was the acceptance Hallie had been waiting for. It was proof that the special bond Hallie had patiently nurtured would never be broken.

Hallie kissed her fingers, then placed them on the picture. "Love you, sweet girl."

Hallie reached for the last stack.

They were the most recent pictures taken two months ago in February. Ahn was in her high chair wearing a party hat, staring at her birthday cake with three brightly lit candles on the tray in front of her. The next one The Colonel had taken of her, Jen, Ben and Roberta—also wearing party hats and clapping as Ahn blew out her candles.

But Hallie kept staring at the image of Ahn holding the stuffed duck Nate had sent her, thinking how Nate was sadly living out that early accusation he'd tossed at her of sending birthday and Christmas presents and making a call now and then. At least he did call, and Jen always told Hallie when he did.

But he didn't call Hallie. And Hallie didn't call him. What was the point?

He'd made his decision when he left for California.

Hallie had just closed the photo album when Buster

raised his head from his usual position lying beside her chair. Seconds later, she and Buster were both on their feet, ready to welcome Ahn for her overnight visit.

After the accident, Hallie didn't think she would ever be happy again. There were still moments when she missed Janet and David so much she would almost double over from the sick feeling in the pit of her stomach.

Then she would remember all of the things that she did have to be thankful for. Ahn, always. Jen and Ben, who had become her family. She still loved her career. Even she and Roberta were so much closer than Hallie ever imagined they could be.

Her life was satisfying. Not perfect, but satisfying.

And she refused to think about who would make it perfect.

THE SCENERY FROM THE DECK of the small beach house he'd rented in Malibu was beautiful, the sun shining on the ocean and the waves lapping at the shore below. But Nate was finding some truth in the fact that you could change your surroundings but still be left with all the same stuff.

Getting far away from Boston hadn't delivered the same exhilaration and freedom he'd felt the first time he cut out and ran. Maybe because then he'd been running from what he wanted to forget. Whereas now he'd been trying to get away from what he couldn't forget.

He'd picked up the phone a dozen times to call

Hallie. But he'd always stopped short of making the connection.

She'd moved on during the past six months. Nate knew that because Ben had become his informant, feeding him updates on what she was doing.

So Nate knew she was doing great without him. That was why it wasn't fair to barge into her life when he still couldn't put a finger on what he had come out here to clear up. Something kept holding him back. And until Nate knew what that something was, he would continue to check on Hallie and Ahn as he'd promised—from a distance and in the background.

Nate walked inside the beach house and picked up the envelope on the kitchen table that held the latest pictures of Ahn Jen had sent him. He'd looked at them a dozen times and every time he did he couldn't believe how much she'd grown.

He missed her like crazy and hated that he'd missed all these recent developments of hers. But he did believe that giving Ahn the gift of Ben and Jen as parents was the best thing he and Hallie could have done for her.

Nate carefully put the pictures back in the envelope and picked up the invitation that had been included with them. As much as he'd like to be at Ahn's first dance recital, he couldn't. But the fact that Jen always invited him let Nate know he was always welcome with or without an invitation. For that he was grateful.

Nate grabbed his keys off the table and headed for the door. He had meetings this afternoon at a studio to discuss a new project he and Dirk were proposing—a behind-the-scenes look into the political process in Washington.

Dirk had several congressmen on board to discuss their tenure in the Capital. And Nate had already talked to Senator Harris, who had also agreed to be interviewed for the documentary. The senator's involvement had led Ben to say he was looking forward to Nate working on the east coast so they could hang out.

Nate hadn't commented on that. But privately he thought it highly unlikely he'd be spending time with the Harrises.

He wouldn't do that to Hallie.

He wouldn't do that to himself.

"Look, Mommy, it's me when I was little baby Ahn."

Ahn was sitting on Hallie's lap at Hallie's kitchen table looking through the photo album Hallie had put together for her.

"And who is with you?" Jen asked from the chair next to them.

"My other mommy and daddy who loved me very, very much, and who are up in heaven always watching over me."

"Always," Hallie assured Ahn.

Ahn kept turning the pages until she found another section she liked. She stopped at the New York trip.

"There's Ba and Ong," she said, pointing to Jen's mom and dad, then she rattled off something to Jen in Vietnamese that Hallie didn't understand. Ahn switched back to English when she pointed to Ben's parents. "And there's Grandpa and Mimi."

Hallie looked over at Jen. "I'm so glad you're teaching Ahn Vietnamese early. That was something Janet and David were planning to do."

"My parents were determined their children were going to be bilingual. Of course, having been born here, I speak better English than I do Vietnamese. But you should hear Ahn talking to my parents on the phone. I wonder if Vietnamese comes so easy for her because that's the first language that was spoken to her."

Ahn turned the page. "There's Berta and Old Poop."

Roberta had made the mistake of calling The Colonel an old poop in front of Ahn. Ahn had called him that since. In fact, they all had—behind his back, of course. Only Ahn could get away with saying it to his face.

"That's me. And that's my Nate," Ahn said when she turned the pages backward until she found the picture of them asleep on the sofa. But she looked up at Hallie with a mischievous grin.

"No. My Nate," Hallie told her and tickled Ahn.

Ahn squealed in delight.

It was a game they used to play for Nate's affection and Ahn had never forgotten it. Nate had always chosen Ahn over Hallie. Looking back on how their lives had unfolded, she had to wonder if that had been a game.

"No, Aunt Hallie. My Nate," Ahn said again, wiggling off Hallie's lap, bored with the pictures and the teasing.

Buster was a willing victim when Ahn sat on the floor beside him. He licked her face.

"My Buster," she said and hugged him before she leaned over with her ear to Buster's mouth.

It was another game Ahn liked to play. When she wanted to do something she thought might be refused, she always blamed it on Buster.

She looked up at Hallie. "Buster says he wants to go watch *Nemo*. Can he?"

"Ask your mommy first," Hallie told her.

Ahn looked up at Jen.

Jen nodded in approval and Ahn and Buster disappeared in the den. There was no reason for Hallie or Jen to go start the movie. Ahn could operate the DVD player better than both of them.

When they left, Hallie rose and placed the album on the bookshelf in the kitchen. She returned with the coffee carafe to refill Jen's cup and her own.

"I can't wait for you and Roberta to see Ahn in her tutu next week," Jen said.

"Old Poop's coming with us," Hallie said.

"I sent Nate an invitation, too, Hallie. I doubt he'll come, but I wanted you to know in case he does."

Hallie sighed. "You might not believe this, but I would be thrilled if Nate came. And not for the reason you're thinking. It has nothing to do with me. It just breaks my heart that Nate is missing so much of Ahn's life. He should be there for her first dance recital, dammit."

"Don't worry," Jen said. "I'll send him a copy of the

video. Believe me, Ben will be the obnoxious father in front with his camera." Jen paused for a second before she said, "Tell me the truth, Hallie. Don't you miss him?"

"Of course I miss him."

"I can't even imagine what you're going through being away from him like this. I panic even if Ben's late getting back from the gym, afraid he's been in some fatal accident." Her hand instantly flew to her mouth. "God, Hallie, what a completely thoughtless thing for me to say to you. I am *so* sorry."

Hallie reached out and took Jen's hand.

"There's no reason to apologize, Jen. In fact, maybe Janet and David's accident is why I have been able to get through Nate leaving. The accident is proof that there are no guarantees in life. I have to accept he isn't coming back and get over it."

"Well, I'm still worried about you. I even felt guilty about Ahn sleeping over tonight. If you weren't taking care of her, you might decide to go out and get laid. I'll tell you right now I'm one woman who would not be able to go six months without a little somethin'-somethin' on the side."

Hallie laughed. "I'll take Ahn any day over a little somethin'-somethin' on the side, Jen."

"Well, maybe that's a good thing," Jen said. "Ahn would have pitched a fit if she hadn't been allowed to come."

"I would have, too. Having Ahn sleep over keeps me

sane. Plus she gives me someone to talk to other than Buster."

"You know very well the only reason you have no one to talk to is of your own choosing, Hallie Weston."

"Maybe so. But I'm not ready yet. Maybe someday I'll date again. But to tell you the truth, the thought of going back to the dating scene and meaningless sex for the sake of it makes me want to throw up."

"Even if the meaningless sex happened when you took a quick weekend trip out to Malibu?"

"Drop it, Jen," Hallie warned. "If Nate ever gets back in my bed, it will be because he wants to be there, not because I pushed him into it like I did before."

"Well, I don't care what you say. I think you need to call him, tell him you're miserable without him and tell him to get his sweet ass home."

"I think that's one of Nate's problems," Hallie said. "He doesn't know what it's like to have a real home. And that's why he can't envision having one."

"Or," Jen said, "maybe the home he did envision was with you and Ahn. Then Ben and I came along and messed that up."

"You did not mess anything up. I don't ever want to hear you say that again. If Nate hadn't thought you and Ben were the right parents for Ahn, he never would have agreed to the readoption. I do know him well enough to know that."

Jen leaned over to hug Hallie.

"I'll tell you something else," Hallie said. "If the only way Nate could see making a home with me was if Ahn stayed in the picture, he did me a big favor by leaving. I'm better off without him."

"And you really feel that way?"

"Absolutely."

She grinned. "Then how soon can I fix you up with that cute new associate Ben just hired?"

Hallie swatted her. "You're impossible."

Ahn came running into the kitchen with Buster loping in behind.

"Buster wants two cookies, one milk."

Jen and Hallie looked at each other and laughed.

"I'll get Buster's cookies," Hallie said.

Jen said, "I'll get Buster's milk."

CHAPTER SEVENTEEN

"YOU HAVEN'T HEARD a word I've said, have you, Nate?"

Nate glanced over at Dirk. They were sitting at an outside café in downtown L.A. eating lunch after their Thursday meeting with another bunch of executives at the studio. And no, Nate hadn't been listening to a word Dirk said.

Nate had been in a foul mood all day. He suspected it would be even worse tomorrow. Ahn would be onstage at her dance recital, and everyone would be there to watch. Everyone except him.

He had arranged for a huge balloon bouquet to be delivered to Ahn today with a card from him. He also planned to call her tomorrow before the recital so he could tell her how proud he was of her. It was keeping in touch with her that counted.

At least Nate told himself that.

"I gotta get this," Dirk said, grabbing his phone from the table and slapping it against his ear.

Nate was glad for the break.

They'd become good friends while working on the documentary, but Dirk had obsessive-compulsive disorder big-time and minutia was his specialty. He'd been talking nonstop since they arrived, another reason Nate had tuned him out. They'd gone over the particulars of their new project beyond the need to ever go over those details again. As soon as Dirk got off the phone, Nate was going to dump him and get the hell out of here.

He glanced around, trying not to eavesdrop on Dirk. An old guy at the intersection caught Nate's eye. As the light turned yellow the man stepped off the curb. From his peripheral vision Nate spied rapid movement and turned to see a car approaching the same intersection going way too fast with no signs of slowing.

Dammit! Didn't the driver see the old man?

"What the hell?" Dirk yelled when Nate jumped up, overturning the table.

Nate made a lunge forward and grabbed the old man by the back of his shirt, spinning him around. The guy fell backward out of the way, but Nate fell forward.

When the car hit him, the impact lifted Nate off his feet and threw him into the air. He landed on the pavement flat on his back with such force it knocked the breath out of him.

Nate struggled to breathe as darkness closed in around him. And the last thing he saw before everything went black was Hallie's beautiful smiling face.

HALLIE HAD HER HEADPHONES on directing the afternoon newscast from the control booth when she had a feeling settle over her that something was wrong. She tried to shake it off, but she couldn't. She finally motioned to her assistant to take over and headed straight to her office.

She grabbed her cell phone from her purse and quickly scrolled to Jen's cell number and punched call. To her relief Jen answered.

"I was just thinking about you," Jen said. "You aren't riding with Roberta and Old Poop tomorrow night are you?"

"No. Why?"

"Because I want you to pack your jammies and sleep over. I don't know why I didn't think to ask you before. But there isn't any sense in you driving back to Boston after the recital. Besides, if you stay over, that will give us a good excuse to go shopping on Saturday."

"One slight problem," Hallie said. "Buster."

"Bring him. You and Buster can stay in the cottage. Ben won't even have to take his allergy medicine."

Hallie hesitated. Thinking about Nate's cottage had thrown her for a second. She shook that off, too.

"Well, I guess Buster would be all right in the cottage while we're at the recital."

"Say yes," Jen urged. "Ahn will be ecstatic."

"Okay. Yes."

"So? What's up? Why did you call?"

Again, Hallie hesitated. There wasn't any reason to worry Jen with the eerie feeling that had come over her. Especially not now that she knew Ahn was safe.

"You know, I can't even remember why I called," Hallie lied. "I'll talk to you later."

"Wait," Jen said. "I wanted to tell you something else. Ahn got a huge balloon bouquet from Nate this morning. Ahn was thrilled. The card said he'd call her before the recital."

"I'm glad he did that for her," Hallie said. "See you tomorrow."

So Nate wasn't coming. His loss. Not theirs.

Hallie dropped her phone back into her purse, refusing to think about Nate one second longer. She was excited about the weekend and she wasn't going to let him not showing up spoil that.

Leaving her desk, Hallie headed back to the control room, her mind already focusing on what she'd always done best—her job. She at least had that satisfaction. For today, that would have to be enough.

THE LAST FACE Nate had seen before he passed out was Hallie's. But the first face Nate saw when he came to was the old man he'd pushed out of the way.

"Thank God you're alive, son," the old man said. "You saved my life."

That thought sobered Nate.

As fast as the darkness had closed in around him earlier, Nate finally stepped forward into the light of clarity.

He'd been running from death.

From his father's death. From David's death. And from his own mortality. Nate still had it all screwed up in his head that a commitment to Hallie would tempt death to take it all away from him. He'd falsely believed that as long as fate placed them together there would be no threat involved. But when the time came to make a conscious *choice* to remain with Hallie, it had scared Nate. He hadn't been willing to leave Hallie behind the way his father had left him and David had left Ahn.

But now Nate knew the truth.

Death hadn't taken his father because he had a family he loved. His father had done exactly what Nate had done when he saw someone in danger—he'd acted on instinct. Just as David's death hadn't been a punishment for loving Janet and Ahn. Accidents happened. Nobody planned for them to happen. Nobody could control whether or not they happened. But they were accidents, not punishments.

He'd been afraid of leaving Hallie behind, yet what had he done?

He'd left her behind anyway.

Unless he started living his life instead of running from death, Nate knew he wasn't going to be any better off than his mother had been spending all those years lying in bed staring at a blank wall.

"Don't try to get up, man," Dirk said, bending over Nate with his cell phone still to his ear. "The ambulance is on the way to take you to the hospital."

Nate sat up anyway.

He was bruised and banged up. But as far as he could tell he was still all in one piece and nothing was broken. He rolled his neck, just to make sure.

"You are one lucky SOB," Dirk said. "Man, if you'd

landed even one foot farther out in the street another car would have hit you."

Yeah, he was one lucky SOB. He loved an incredible woman, and, with a little more luck, she still loved him. The second he was medically cleared, he was heading to the airport to find out.

HALLIE STOOD AT THE BACK of Winchester's community theater, scanning the crowd for a familiar face. She saw Roberta first and made her way down the aisle to where Roberta sat with The Colonel.

Hallie pardoned her way into the middle of the row to take the empty seat beside Roberta just as the lights in the theater were going down.

"Jen's backstage with Ahn," Roberta said. "She said she'd find us after the program." But Roberta couldn't resist scolding Hallie when she said, "Why are you late?"

"Traffic," Hallie explained.

"That's the reason The Colonel and I left an hour early."

Hallie groaned inwardly. But she was not going to let Roberta ruin Ahn's recital for her. She hadn't been late, thank you very much. She'd been right on time. And Roberta could just get over it.

"Welcome to our program tonight," the instructor in charge of the program said as she stepped in front of the microphone. "On behalf of all of our dancers, I want you to know we couldn't be more pleased to see this theater filled with family and friends."

Hallie leaned forward in her seat looking for Ben. She smiled when she found him exactly where Jen said he'd be, crouched in front of the stage, his video camera already poised and ready.

The instructor left the stage and the music started.

A mild disturbance sounded at the end of their row. Hallie purposely ignored whoever it was slowly inching toward the only vacant seat, which was right beside her. She was too intent on finding Ahn when a group of adorable pink tutus flooded the stage and everyone clapped in approval.

"There she is. Third from the left," Hallie whispered to Roberta as the person sat. "Isn't she the most beautiful thing you've ever seen?"

"She's one of the most beautiful things I've ever seen."

Hallie froze.

She'd know that voice anywhere.

When Hallie turned her head, Nate said, "I'm looking at the other most beautiful thing I've ever seen right now."

Someone behind them shushed Nate.

They looked back at the stage in time to see Ahn lift her arms above her head and do a three-year-old's version of a perfect pirouette. Hallie kept her eyes straight ahead, her heart pounding and her head spinning with anticipation at what Nate sitting beside her might mean. Finally, Hallie found the courage to ask.

"How long are you home?"

"Forever," Nate said. "I promise."

Hallie didn't pull away when Nate's fingers closed tightly around hers. The man she loved had promised her forever as they watched their amazing niece make her debut as a ballerina—together—the way it should be.

The world might not be perfect.

But for Hallie, this moment was.

* * * * *

HARLEQUIN Super Romance®

COMING NEXT MONTH

Available November 9, 2010

#1668 THAT CHRISTMAS FEELING
Brenda Novak, Kathleen O'Brien, Karina Bliss

#1669 THE BEST LAID PLANS
Sarah Mayberry

#1670 A MARINE FOR CHRISTMAS
A Little Secret
Beth Andrews

#1671 A LOT LIKE CHRISTMAS
Going Back
Dawn Atkins

#1672 THE MOON THAT NIGHT
Single Father
Helen Brenna

#1673 LIFE REWRITTEN
Suddenly a Parent
Margaret Watson

LARGER-PRINT BOOKS!
GET 2 FREE LARGER-PRINT NOVELS PLUS
2 FREE GIFTS!

HARLEQUIN®

Super Romance®

Exciting, emotional, unexpected!

YES! Please send me 2 FREE LARGER-PRINT Harlequin® Superromance® novels and my 2 FREE gifts (gifts are worth about $10). After receiving them, if I don't wish to receive any more books, I can return the shipping statement marked "cancel." If I don't cancel, I will receive 6 brand-new novels every month and be billed just $5.44 per book in the U.S. or $5.99 per book in Canada. That's a saving of at least 13% off the cover price! It's quite a bargain! Shipping and handling is just 50¢ per book.* I understand that accepting the 2 free books and gifts places me under no obligation to buy anything. I can always return a shipment and cancel at any time. Even if I never buy another book from Harlequin, the two free books and gifts are mine to keep forever.

139/339 HDN E5PS

Name _____ (PLEASE PRINT) _____

Address _____ Apt. # _____

City _____ State/Prov. _____ Zip/Postal Code _____

Signature (if under 18, a parent or guardian must sign)

Mail to the **Harlequin Reader Service:**
IN U.S.A.: P.O. Box 1867, Buffalo, NY 14240-1867
IN CANADA: P.O. Box 609, Fort Erie, Ontario L2A 5X3

Not valid for current subscribers to Harlequin Superromance Larger-Print books.

**Are you a current subscriber to Harlequin Superromance books
and want to receive the larger-print edition?
Call 1-800-873-8635 today!**

* Terms and prices subject to change without notice. Prices do not include applicable taxes. N.Y. residents add applicable sales tax. Canadian residents will be charged applicable provincial taxes and GST. Offer not valid in Quebec. This offer is limited to one order per household. All orders subject to approval. Credit or debit balances in a customer's account(s) may be offset by any other outstanding balance owed by or to the customer. Please allow 4 to 6 weeks for delivery. Offer available while quantities last.

Your Privacy: Harlequin Books is committed to protecting your privacy. Our Privacy Policy is available online at www.eHarlequin.com or upon request from the Reader Service. From time to time we make our lists of customers available to reputable third parties who may have a product or service of interest to you. If you would prefer we not share your name and address, please check here. ☐

Help us get it right—We strive for accurate, respectful and relevant communications. To clarify or modify your communication preferences, visit us at www.ReaderService.com/consumerschoice.

HSRLP10R

HARLEQUIN®

A Romance

FOR EVERY MOOD™

Spotlight on

Inspirational

Wholesome romances
that touch the heart and soul.

See the next page
to enjoy a sneak peek from
the Love Inspired® Suspense
inspirational series.

*See below for a sneak peek from
our inspirational line, Love Inspired® Suspense*

*Enjoy this heart-stopping excerpt from
RUNNING BLIND
by top author Shirlee McCoy,
available November 2010!*

**The mission trip to Mexico was supposed to be an
adventure. But the thrill turns sour when Jenna Dougherty
and her roommate Magdalena are kidnapped.**

"It's okay. I'm here to help." The voice was as deep as the
darkness, but Jenna Dougherty didn't believe the lie. She
could do nothing but lie still as hands slid down her arms,
felt the rope around her wrists.

"I'm going to use a knife to cut you free, Jenna. Hold
still."

The cold blade of a knife pressed close to her head before
her gag fell away.

"I—" she started, but her mouth was dry, and she could
do nothing but suck in air.

"Shhh. Whatever needs to be said can be said when
we're out of here." Nick spoke quietly, his hand gentle on
her cheek. There and gone as he sliced through the ropes on
her wrists and ankles.

He pulled her upright. "Come on. We may be on
borrowed time."

"I can't leave my friend," Jenna rasped out.

"There's no one here. Just us."

"She has to be here." Jenna took a step away.

"There's no one here. Let's go before that changes."

"It's dark. Maybe if we find a light…"

"What did you say?"

"We need to turn on the light. I can't leave until I know that—"

"What can you see, Jenna?"

"Nothing."

"No shadows? No light?"

"No."

"It's broad daylight. There's light spilling in from the window I climbed in through. You can't see it?"

She went cold at his words.

"I can't see anything."

"You've got a nasty bruise on your forehead. Maybe that has something to do with it." His fingers traced the tender flesh on her forehead.

"It doesn't matter *how* it happened. I'm blind!"

Can Nick help Jenna find her friend or will chasing this trail have Jenna running blindly again into danger?

Find out in RUNNING BLIND, available in November 2010 only from Love Inspired Suspense.

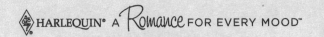